Knot a Midlife Crisis

DAISY EMORY

TURBO KITTEN INDUSTRIES

To Avery for loving me without limits and never giving up on us.

CHAPTER 1

Brooklyn

"WHAT DO you mean you're cutting me off?" I asked my father, my brows nearly touching my hairline.

Dad sat at his mahogany desk, the gorgeous, pure blue Lake Tahoe water and snowcapped mountains visible through the double doors behind him. Those doors led to a patio with a full bar, chairs, a couple tables, and most of my teenage and adult memories. When he was out of town on business, I could be found in one of those chairs, soaking up sun or breathing in the chilly winter air to clear my head. Winter was my favorite time because of the snow we always got.

Dad looked up from the papers he was signing, his desk constantly piled high with documents, to the point that only those sitting across from him knew it was mahogany. "Exactly what I said. Until you find a pack, I'm cutting you off financially. You can forget that ridiculous vacation you planned. We all know you're just dealing with a midlife crisis."

Laughter was probably not the response he expected, but that was what he got.

His brows furrowed, he steepled his fingers, and cleared his throat. "Brooklyn, you're clearly not taking this seriously."

After wiping the tears from my face, I said, "Dad, I've been financially independent since I was seventeen. My trip was paid for by *me*. I haven't taken a penny from you since I became an adult. I know you're used to Annabelle and Norma taking you for everything that they can, but I'm not like my sisters." I wasn't like my sisters in so many ways that it hurt my brain to even try to list them. Not only was I not a married mother with a pack, I wasn't ever, *ever* dependent on my parents' money as an adult.

His eyes widened and he started furiously searching on his computer.

Standing, I said, "Search your records all you want, Dad, but you're only going to prove that I'm right."

He stopped his search, returned to his stoicism, and said, "Be that as it may, you have a duty as an omega, to this family, to find your pack and produce heirs."

Like a barb to the heart, I cringed. Did he not realize that I was trying? Did he not know how many apps, agencies, and other sources I'd utilized to try to find my fated mates? Hundreds of dates. Hundreds of rejections.

I wanted to find the men who completed me more than I wanted my business to succeed, but since they seemed to not exist, I focused on my business. Plus, I hated the idea that it was my *duty* to have kids. Sure, I wanted them, but it was my body and it was ultimately my choice.

"I'm sorry to be a disappointment," I snapped and spun

on my heel. "I'm going on my vacation, and there's nothing you can do to stop me."

"Brooklyn!" he called after me, but I ignored him.

Once in my room, I resumed packing my bag, throwing in the teeny tiny bikini I'd purchased recently for this occasion. Maybe, I'd just find some men who might be willing to wait until my next heat to impregnate me without any additional strings.

Sure, I wanted a pack, a group of alphas to knot me when I needed, or wanted, it. A group to treat me like a queen. My mother had had three alphas and one beta, the men I considered my fathers, who had pampered her. They had treated her like she was the only woman on earth and growled at anyone who ventured too close to their sun.

I wanted all of that. I wanted men who cherished me.

However, I also wanted to provide an heir, like my annoying sisters, that my parents would dote on and love. One I could snuggle with and spoil.

Honestly, even if I never had a child, though, I really wanted to find an alpha, at least one, who loved me.

Somewhere out there, there had to be an alpha for me. Just one. Of the billions in the world. There had to be one who would want me.

Right?

"What do you mean the counts are off?" I asked Marcus, my right-hand man in the business. He was a single alpha without a pack, having never found one growing up. The way he flinched or cowered when he heard growling made me think he'd experienced some type of abuse, but it wasn't my place to ask, and it wouldn't be fair to open up old wounds unnecessarily. He did his job fantastically, and so I went out of my way to provide him with a working environment that was void of growly alphas.

"We were supposed to order two hundred, but we only ordered twenty," he repeated.

Slapping a hand over my face, I asked, "How long will it take to get the rest?"

"The printer said they could put a rush order on them for an extra fifty dollars and get them to us by next week."

The product was supposed to launch next week, once I returned from my vacation, so that would be pushing it close, but we could always put a note that it would take one to two business days for order processing on the website if necessary. This new product was one I was very passionate about, a journal with positive affirmation quotes and reminders that omegas could do more than just be broodmares. My social media had exploded when I mentioned what I was working on, so we'd rushed it faster than normal.

"Do it. And order an extra fifty just to be safe," I ordered him.

"Yes, ma'am," he said in a soft voice. "You sure you're not an alpha? That was almost a bark."

Shit. I'd upset him.

"I'm sorry. I'm not mad at you and I didn't mean to take it

out on you. Why don't you handle the order and take the rest of the day off?" I didn't bother responding to his question because we all knew that only males could be alphas and I was just stressed.

"I'm okay. Thank you for apologizing. I'm going to get this order placed and go check on marketing to see how they are doing with the advertisement images. Now, I want you to get off the phone. Don't worry about work, and focus on finding yourself an alpha to ease some of that tension."

I laughed and shook my head. "Marcus, you and I both know I'm a bit old to search for a pack."

"Stranger things have happened. Like an omega owning a million-dollar company without the backing of her rich family."

"Touché."

"Don't forget to ask for sunscreen! We know you burn easily and asking them to spread sunscreen on you will be a great pickup line!"

"I'm hanging up now," I grumbled. Marcus was as worried about my sex life as my family.

"Don't worry about work. I'll take care of it while you're gone for a week. Bye!"

I stared at the phone and shook my head. He was something else, but he was also one of my best friends at this point.

Was that sad? Was it sad that my assistant was my best friend? I'd had a few girl friends, but it got harder and harder to maintain relationships once they found their packs and started having kids.

Maybe it was petty, but seeing them so happy always reminded me of how unhappy I was.

This trip, I would force myself to do all the fun things and have fun. No more holding back. "I am a badass, smart, and beautiful woman. I will make this life into my dream, no matter how long it takes."

"Did you even listen to your father?" Mom asked as I dragged my suitcase down the stairs.

Sighing at her or growling wouldn't phase her. Instead, I smiled and said, "Yes, Mother. I listened to his ridiculousness."

"Ridiculousness?" she asked.

Stopping halfway down the stairs, I turned to face her and said, "You know I don't take money from you and haven't since I left. However, he didn't."

She pursed her lips. "Hm."

My mother was well aware of my accomplishments, and that I hadn't taken a single cent from them since I graduated.

"I appreciate your concern. Please let him know that I do understand my *duty,* and I am not just ignoring it." As much as it pained me to mention it, I still said it.

She sighed and ran a hand down her face. "My husband has developed baby fever again."

Grandbaby fever.

"I'm sorry," she said and set her hand on my shoulder.

Mother was at least three inches taller than my five foot four frame, but a dwarf when it came to her mate. Her golden hair glowed in the overhead lights and her bright green eyes seemed to glow with a fire of their own. One that I remembered seeing quite frequently as a young adult when in trouble.

"Mom, I don't hate you or him. I know that he has done his best since ..." Since my other fathers died in a car accident four years ago, leaving him the sole alpha in the family.

Mom dropped her head a moment before raising it and smiling warmly at me. "I hope you have a ton of fun on your vacation. You've been putting a lot of hours into your business and are well overdue for a vacation. Who knows, maybe you'll find a handsome man or two to take your mind off of things."

"Fingers crossed, Mom. Fingers crossed," I said with a smile.

She kissed me on the cheek and slid a credit card into my hand. "Don't limit yourself. Spend whatever you want while you are on this trip. Buy all the things, go on all the excursions, get drunk every night. Do not hold back."

I wanted to give her the credit card back, but she gave me her famous don't-talk-back, expression, so I slid it into my pocket and hugged her. "I love you, Mom."

She hugged me back. "I love you too, my eldest. I know that you will come into your own when you are ready."

"Maybe I am having a midlife crisis," I whispered.

"Well, we all experience it in different ways," she said.

I could see the evidence of her midlife crisis, a cherry red motorcycle that sat collecting dust, if I just went into the garage. She'd driven that thing for a full year before my dads convinced her to hang the keys up for good. Their nerves couldn't handle her driving a motorcycle where they couldn't protect her.

"What if I never find them?" I asked softly, eyes on the ground.

She set her hand on my arm and hummed. "I'm certain there is someone for you out there, Brooklyn. You are beautiful and smart, and any man would be lucky to get ten seconds of your time, let alone win you as a mate. However, even if you don't find a pack or an alpha, you are doing a lot to show the world what omegas are capable of in the business world. I know I don't tell you often enough, but I am proud of you and what you have accomplished. Growing your business from pennies to millions was no small feat, and you continue to surprise me with your expansions and amazing products. I see all the positive comments from omegas who purchase through you and how much of a difference you make in their lives."

If she knew what my next move was, she'd probably faint. Not even Marcus knew what I was planning.

Tears leaked down my cheeks and I sniffled before hugging her. "Thank you."

"Now, go on your vacation and have the best midlife crisis ever!" she yelled.

After wiping my face, I said, "It's not a midlife crisis."

The protest was halfhearted as I grabbed my suitcase and headed to the front door, where one of our drivers had a car running to take me to the airport.

I put my mask on as I climbed into the car. Some people thought it strange to see a woman wearing a respirator mask, but there were so many people who smelled downright foul or sour that I had started wearing it whenever I could.

I'd almost thrown up in an airplane the last time I'd not worn one.

After dealing with so many people who constantly smelled bad, I couldn't imagine the rumors that your pack smelled sinfully delicious were true. I supposed they would have to at least smell decent, or it would be hard to stay with them, let alone sleep with them.

I'd had to wear the mask the entire time I was in the heat clinic. After a single trip to the clinic, I'd begged my family to build me a separate building on the property that I used to isolate myself during my heats. The pain was almost debilitating, but since I hadn't found my pack yet, there was no other cure,.

Thankfully, my heat wasn't due for two more weeks, so I could enjoy this week and then come back without issue.

In just a few hours, I would be basking in the sun with the warm ocean splashing against my toes.

CHAPTER 2

Buck

One of the perks of being a pack of millionaires was having our own personal jet. I'd spent a lot of time in cramped seats and taking cheap flights when I was younger. When I'd started my coaching business, one of my goals had been to get a jet and now, I was taking full advantage of it.

As expected, Tyler immediately turned music on and started playing the air guitar. The musician couldn't stand silence or lack of music in general.

I poured glasses of champagne for everyone, more than excited to go on vacation and finally have some time to relax.

"How long until we take off?" Kirk asked in his deep, growling tone as he took the offered glass from my hand. The former military man loved his strict routines.

"We'll be taking off in about ten minutes," the pilot said from the cockpit.

I hadn't realized he had the door open and could hear us.

Tyler took the other champagne glass from me and held it

up. "A toast! To all of us for being awesome and to finally reuniting!"

We touched glasses and drank the champagne.

"It is good to have you both back by my side," Kirk admitted as he looked at his glass.

I set a hand on his shoulder and squeezed.

Normally, once a pack was formed, you didn't separate. But life had thrown a few curveballs at us, like me joining the football league and then getting injured, Tyler going viral and going on tours around the world, and Kirk getting deployed overseas.

"All that matters is that we're together now," I said. We'd been back together for six months, but this was the first time we'd had time to do anything together since I'd been so busy.

"And we're going to find our omega. I can feel it," Tyler said with a nod.

Kirk scoffed. "I doubt we'll ever find our omega, but I would settle for some action."

"We're going to a beach destination. There's going to be plenty of women to choose from," Tyler said confidently.

Not that he ever had an issue finding some tail.

The bastard had swum in it while on tour. He was lucky that he was a beta and didn't have the alpha urges Kirk and I did. Without a knot, it was also easier for him to sleep around.

"We're ready to take off," the pilot announced. "Please fasten your seatbelts."

Kirk immediately obeyed, while Tyler and I took our time pouring a second glass before buckling in.

Maybe Tyler was right, maybe we were finally going to find our omega.

There had been one girl in high school that I'd thought smelled better than the others, but her combative attitude had turned me off at the time. Now, I didn't mind a woman who had some bite to her, but the chances of seeing her again after more than twenty years, were slim to none. She likely had a pack and several babies.

"Why are you scowling so much? We're supposed to be celebrating," Kirk reminded me.

"You remember that girl in high school, the one who always talked back to us and stopped us from putting Mr. Hunter's car in the gym?" I asked.

Kirk's brow furrowed and he tilted his head to look up at the ceiling of the jet while he thought. "That was so long ago, I barely remember it, but I think I know who you're talking about. What about her?"

I ran a hand down my face and took a big drink. "Nothing, just getting nostalgic in my old age, I guess."

"It's a midlife crisis, not old age," Tyler countered.

"I am *not* having a midlife crisis," I growled.

He just smiled back at me.

"Asshole."

Once in the air, I relaxed and watched the scenery as we flew above it. So many people. Millions of people. Yet, we hadn't found the one omega we were meant to.

Perhaps fate hated us.

Or we'd all used up our luck in our jobs.

Maybe my nose was broken from all the hits I'd taken in football. Kirk had broken his nose at least five times in the military, so that could explain his being broken, too. As a beta, Tyler's nose wasn't as sensitive as ours, so maybe ...

No. I knew it was just that we hadn't yet found her. The one who would complete us. The one who would smell the best. My fathers had explained it to me, but it was hard to accept that one woman would smell immensely better than the others. It was hard to imagine that as soon as I got a good whiff of her scent that I'd immediately start growling at any other men who even looked at her.

Maybe that was just how my fathers had reacted, despite them assuring me that I would be the same.

Tyler's dig about going through a midlife crisis had stung more than it should have because, unbeknownst to them, my mother had berated me for an hour about it this morning. She was certain I had shunned my omega and was hiding from her. She even went so far as to threaten me to get me to expose who the girl was, so that she could offer the girl retribution for me discarding her.

Thankfully, my fathers had taken the phone from her at that point and wished me a good vacation.

"You smell annoyed," Kirk commented with his eyes closed.

I sighed. "I can't keep anything from you, can I?"

He opened a single eye and said, "What are you hiding? I thought we didn't hide anything from each other?"

"Except snacks," Tyler amended.

"Mom gave me a hard time this morning," I admitted. "Same as usual."

"She must have called mine, too, because she harassed me as well," Tyler grumbled.

"Mine said she thinks I'm meant to be solo and you're preventing me from finding my omega," Kirk said and closed his eye again.

"Wow, that's harsh," I whispered.

"She apologized as soon as she said it. They're all freaking out because they want more grandbabies," Kirk said before his tone dropped into a mimicry of his mother. "It's not enough to just make money, you know. You need a family or you're going to end up alone," Kirk said.

Tyler rolled his eyes. "Because six isn't enough for Stacy?"

Stacy, Kirk's mother, was always holding one of her grandchildren, or teaching them etiquette, or some other spoiling act like buying them ponies or horses. They had a full stable just for the grandchildren's horses.

"I'm pretty sure she would have dozens of grandbabies if it were up to her. The fact that I, the second oldest, haven't given her even one is her frustration."

Yes, and his youngest brother had given her three already.

"Well, mine just said she I hadn't gone on tour solo; what if my omega had been in the audience but because you weren't with me, we missed it. She constantly rubs my beta status in my face. I'd love to find an omega, even a fake one, to take her home to shut her up."

He should have sounded mad, but Tyler just sounded defeated.

"Sorry! I totally became the Debbie downer. I'm glad you two are back with me, and that we're going to have an entire week at this beach resort, where we can focus on reigniting our bonds. If we find our omega, great, but it's not my focus this trip. If we really want to try finding her, I'm not opposed to using an agency. I hear there are some pretty good ones for those of us with money to weed out the gold diggers."

That had been another concern for me, trying to find someone who wanted *us*, and not just because we were loaded.

I wanted someone who wanted us for us.

Why was that so hard to find?

CHAPTER 3

Brooklyn

STEPPING OFF THE PLANE, I was immediately pummeled by the heat, making me wish I'd worn shorts instead of pants, but the airplanes were always so cold.

Dragging my suitcase behind me, I was glad that at least I didn't have to go wait for a checked bag. Initially, I had wanted to pack another bag, but decided against it to simplify things.

As I walked by the dozen people waiting in baggage claim and out to an empty curb for taxis, I knew I had made the right decision.

The taxi driver loaded my bag while I climbed inside, and quickly took me to the resort.

The resort was huge and right on the coast, with two private beaches only accessible to guests, a pool, two spas, three restaurants, a bar, and outdoor activities. The best part of the resort was their rule that no children were allowed, so I wouldn't have to deal with the pain of seeing families.

"Thank you for the ride," I said to the taxi driver and handed him cash for a tip.

He touched his hat and nodded. "Thank you. Enjoy your stay."

After retrieving my bag, I walked by the valet boys and inside the entrance. Even though I was going to be surrounded by people, I removed my mask. It would be bearable now, and if someone smelled too offensive, I would just vacate the area.

The lobby of the resort was open and airy, with plenty of seating for guests to relax in. The floor-to-ceiling windows offered sweeping views of the ocean, and the natural light streaming in created a bright and inviting atmosphere. The décor was modern and stylish, with a focus on clean lines and neutral colors. There was a concierge desk where guests could ask for directions or recommendations and sign up for excursions, plus a gift shop where they could purchase souvenirs.

At the concierge desk, a woman in her late twenties with a tight bun smiled warmly at me. "Welcome in. What name is the reservation under?"

"Brooklyn," I answered, finishing my walk to the desk, and let go of my suitcase once I was sure it would remain upright. "Brooklyn Vanderman."

She typed it in and nodded. "Checking in today and checking out on the seventeenth. Wonderful, you'll be here for a full week, which will give you plenty of time to take advantage of all of our amazing offerings here in our resort." After grabbing two keycards and a pamphlet, she reached into a small fridge behind her and grabbed a bottle of champagne.

I almost told her I didn't need two keycards, but didn't feel like explaining or getting the sympathetic look I always received.

"You can take the elevator just to the left to the fifth floor. This champagne is complimentary, a welcome gift for you staying with us. You will find glasses in your room on your coffee table when you enter. Please do not hesitate to reach out if you need anything. Our room service kitchen is open twenty-four hours a day."

That was definitely good to know.

"Thank you," I said and saluted her with the pamphlet.

There were no elevators open, so I pushed the button and waited patiently for one to arrive.

"I'm starving!" a man yelled as he entered through the main doors.

"Yeah, let's go change and then get some dinner," another male commented.

I turned and my eyes widened. Three men stood at the concierge desk in swim shorts and nothing else, showing off their tattoos and bodies.

One of the men was tall and muscular, with a chiseled jawline, vibrant green eyes, and a five o'clock shadow. He rolled his eyes at his friend beside him, who was flirting with the concierge clerk who had checked me in.

The man flirting with the concierge clerk had an athletic build with broad shoulders and a narrow waist. His light brown hair looked styled, even though they'd clearly come from the beach.

The tallest of them had to be at least six foot four, with a thick neck and a square jaw covered in a dark brown beard. He was covered in a layer of fluff that only made his beefy body look more muscular, like a powerlifter. I bet he could throw me around easily. His dark eyes surveyed their surroundings in a way that reminded me of my father, who'd been in the military. Always on alert and ready to leap into action.

All three of them looked somewhat familiar, but I couldn't place them. The elevator opened, preventing further inspection.

The elevator moved silently and smoothly up to the fifth floor and it didn't take me long to find my assigned room. The room was decorated in a modern style with a king-sized bed, a flatscreen TV, and a minibar. The bathroom had a walk-in shower and a Jacuzzi tub. The room and bathroom had beach-inspired art that gave them some nice brightness.

The best part was my room had a balcony overlooking the ocean. Opening the balcony doors, I closed my eyes, and let the warm evening air blow my hair back. The salty tang filled my nostrils in a pleasant way, and the sound of the waves crashing against the shore eased the tension filling my body.

Leaving the door open so I could hear the waves and smell the ocean air, I went to the bed and fell onto my back.

However, my stomach chose that moment to remind me it was empty and needed food.

I had wanted to go check out the beach first, but getting food was more of a priority. With a groan, I stood, grabbed my suitcase, and tossed it on the bed to grab a change of clothes and my makeup bag.

I had made sure to buy waterproof makeup for this trip specifically. My mascara was always waterproof, but I wanted to make sure that my eyeshadow and eyeliner stayed perfectly in place as well.

After ensuring my makeup was done to my liking, I put on my bikini and then a tropical sundress over the top. I wanted to look nice while at dinner, but also be able to take the dress off and go to the beach right after. I also put my hair in a ponytail so the wind wouldn't blow it around when I went outside.

Grabbing the tote bag Mom had given me for the trip, I filled it with a beach towel the hotel provided, sunscreen even though it would be getting dark soon, and my earbuds so I could listen to music if I wanted to. Though, I quite enjoyed the simple sound of the waves.

Satisfied with my appearance, I slipped on some rhinestone studded sandals and made my way to one of the restaurants within the resort.

Thankfully, there was no wait and they took me to a table near the bar area. The restaurant entrance was decorated with tropical plants and the interior was full of natural light thanks to large windows allowing a view of the ocean. The menu featured fresh, local ingredients and the dishes were creative and beautifully presented in the pictures.

"A drink, ma'am?" a lithe female waitress with platinum blonde hair asked with a smile.

"Lemon Drop, please and an appetizer of oysters," I requested with a return smile.

She nodded. "Excellent choices. I'll get those both right away for you, while you review the menu for your dinner selection. I'm Ana, and I'll be taking care of you, so don't hesitate to raise your hand if you need me."

"Thank you."

Despite the restaurant being busy, the atmosphere was relaxed and inviting with minimal sound. They must have used white noise machines to keep the voices of others drowned out. It was excellently done.

Once my drink came out, I sipped it and surveyed the other patrons. Most were omegas with their packs, as expected, but there were a few groups of males without an omega amongst them.

The trio from the lobby were there as well, now dressed in jeans and t-shirts, but they were talking to a woman. She looked a bit frazzled, her cheeks were slightly pink, and her gaze darted to her lap often. Were they trying to court her?

They really did look familiar, but no matter how hard I racked my brain, I could not recall where I knew them from.

I hadn't realized I was staring so intently until the beefy one caught me and gave me a wide smile.

Instead of immediately averting my gaze, admitting I was embarrassed, I just tilted my head to the side and squinted.

He mimicked my gesture, which made me smile.

The green-eyed one turned to see what his friend was looking at and when his eyes landed on mine, they widened.

Was that ... recognition?

The woman noticed their distractedness, searching for what it was, and gave me a glare. She flipped her hair over her shoulder and reached out a hand to touch the flirty one on the arm.

The hair flip was a common gesture, sending your scent into their nostrils to entice them.

Strangely, the green-eyed one did not react at all.

"Have you made your decision?" Ana asked.

Oh, I had definitely made a decision to interact with that pack, but not about my dinner selection.

"What do you suggest? I'm not a picky eater and this is my first time here," I said and closed my menu, giving her a soft smile as I met her eyes.

She brightened and I wondered again about my pheromones. For whatever reason, I was able to make other omegas happy. It was a phenomenon I hadn't heard discussed often, but it made me wonder if all omegas could do it, or if it was only a few of us. I knew I could calm some alphas down and that my fated alphas' tempers would be quelled by me. Was it a special talent of mine?

"I recommend the salmon. It's cooked to perfection and the sides are divine as well."

"I'll have that." I handed her my menu and she hurried off to put in my order.

The urge to look back at the trio was immense, but I forced myself to look the opposite way so as not to upset the omega with them. I wasn't a homewrecker, and although I wanted my pack, I wouldn't go about getting them in a devious way.

A male sitting alone at a table across the room caught me looking and stood.

Shit. I hadn't wanted to attract attention that fast. Still, I gave him my best smile as he approached.

"Hello, are you eating alone?"

That was a creepy question, but ...

"Ah, yes, I currently am. It appears you are as well."

He nodded. "Would you care if I join you?"

I wanted to smell him first, but he was too far away, plus I should be nice. "Sure," I replied, sounding much happier about it than I truly was.

Someone growled behind me, but I didn't bother to look.

The man snapped his fingers at Ana. "Move my meal to here."

Anger reared its head at his finger snap and order. The waitress was a human being just like him and not someone he could order around like that.

She brought over his plate. "Here you go."

"Thank you," I said before he could.

She nodded, gave him a scowl he couldn't see, and went over to the trio.

Following her with my eyes, I realized that the green-eyed man was glaring at the guy sitting across from me.

Did they know each other?

"I'm John, and you are?"

Not interested. "Brooklyn," I answered.

"So, is there a reason you aren't packed up yet?" he asked bluntly.

Using my drink as an excuse to delay my response was the only way to keep from snapping at him. "I just haven't found my pack yet," I replied.

"So, are you looking for a pack or are you interested in just a mate?" he questioned, leaning forward with a hopeful expression.

His scent blew across the table and I nearly gagged. Oh,

no. No. No. He did not smell good *at all*. It was like ant poison and rotting food. He was possibly the grossest smelling man I'd met yet. How could one person smell so terrible? I felt bad for him, I really did.

Rubbing my nose and sniffling to hide my disgust, I lied. "I'm holding out hope to find a pack still."

He leaned back and sighed. "Seems to be the way of my life. Well, at least I can enjoy a meal with you tonight."

Hopefully, it would be a quick meal.

I finished my drink and Ana immediately brought me another. "Thank you," I said with a sincerity I hoped she recognized.

"Was your meal to your liking? Do you need anything, sir?" she asked him. He had scarfed down the rest of his food while I'd finished my drink.

"It was a bit lacking in flavor, but what can you expect from a resort restaurant? I'd like a beer, please. Whatever local IPA you have on tap." He wiped his mouth with his napkin and set it on the table beside his plate.

She took his plate and nodded, still smiling despite his rudeness. "I'll get that for you right away. Ma'am, your food will be out shortly."

"Thank you, Ana."

She perked at me remembering her name and quickly left.

He started talking about himself, bragging about his t-shirt business or something, but I tuned him out, nodding along like I was paying attention and trying to breathe through his stench.

"Do you know the pack to our side?" he asked, jarring me out of my thoughts.

Looking at the pack he likely meant would be rude since I didn't know if that was the one he meant. "Which pack?" I asked. "There are several here."

"The one to your left. Two of the men keep glaring at me and looking at us." Ana brought his beer and he didn't even say thank you.

"I'm not sure," I admitted.

"Hm," he grumbled and took a drink from his beer, some of it sloshing down his chin.

Do not throw up on the man, I ordered myself. *You can make it through your meal and then refuse to talk to him again.*

"Guys like that have all the luck," he grumbled and licked his lips as he leered at the woman with them.

I'd been insulted in several ways, but this was a new one, even for me.

"I don't think they're an official pack yet, so you might have a chance with her," I said and shrugged a shoulder.

"Here's your meal. Please let me know if you need anything else," Ana said as she set my plate before me.

"Another drink, please," I ordered and drained the last of my second drink. I knew I needed to slow down, but this guy stressed me out and it hadn't even been an hour in his company.

He resumed talking about himself and complaining about the trio near us while I ate.

I was fairly certain his voice was loud enough for the trio to hear, but so far, they hadn't come over. Maybe they felt bad for the guy, clearly in his late forties, single, and without a pack to even help him through things.

"So, would you like to come back to my room?" he asked suddenly.

I choked on the salmon in my mouth.

He stood and slapped my back, succeeding in hurting me instead of helping me. Ana rushed over and he snapped at her, "Did you not remove all the bones?"

My loveless life flashed before my eyes and I almost laughed at the absurdity of dying by choking on salmon because this loser asked me to his room.

Large arms wrapped around me from behind and successfully gave me the Heimlich maneuver. The salmon shot out of my mouth and right into the loser's beer glass.

CHAPTER 4

Kirk

"Are you alright?" I asked the woman. She was small, beautiful, and busty, and had almost died because the moron next to me hadn't thought to give her the Heimlich. If I'd been a little later, she might not have made it. I'd seen her lips turning blue and had reacted on instinct.

She clutched my forearm that was still wrapped around her middle, shaking slightly. "I-I think so."

The reject of an alpha before me sneered down at his beer now with the piece of food I had dislodged from her throat. "Waitress! Get me a new beer."

The woman in my arms growled, straightened, and shoved my forearm away from her body.

I could have stopped her, but I was curious what she planned to do. My body was tensed, ready to come to her aid, if necessary.

She stepped right up into the other man's personal space and glared up at him, her head coming to his chin. "She is a human being just like you! Not a servant! I almost died because you didn't know how to save me and now, you're yelling at her like it's her fault the salmon is in your drink when she didn't do anything wrong. You even accused her of not removing bones when you know damn well, she isn't the chef. Do you have no respect for others?"

His brows furrowed and he glared down at her. "Listen here, *omega*, you better lower your voice when you talk to—"

Fury at his attitude towards her filled me and a growl ripped out of me before I thought to even do it. "Shut up. She's one hundred percent right, and I don't like your attitude towards her *or* the waitress."

Despite the growl, he didn't flinch or cower. Was I off my game? Did I need to work on my growl? Had I become ... soft?

"So, you do know them," he said to her, ignoring me, and scoffed. "I should have figured. There's no way you're still single at your age unless you're barren or a total bitch. Though, it seems you might be, since your scent is so sour."

She flinched as though he had physically slapped her and took a step back.

My fist connected with his jaw as I moved between them. My instincts to protect her were so strong that I didn't have time to consider anything before reacting.

He fell to one knee, clutching his face.

I pushed the woman behind me to safety. I didn't want to get blood on her pretty tropical dress.

Buck took her arm and gently pulled her back farther in case we started brawling.

"What the hell, man!" he stood up, but noticed Buck at my side now, realized our full foot of height difference as well as physique, and quickly reevaluated the situation. "Whatever, this old pud isn't worth it."

Before I could hit him again, the omega stepped between Buck & I, and kicked him right in the balls.

He fell to his knees with a yelp, clutching himself, eyes clenched shut against the pain.

"Fuck you!" she yelled, her shoulders rising and falling rapidly as she panted.

Laughter boomed out of me while the man groaned. This spicy omega was so interesting.

The waitress, Ana, walked around the man and approached the omega. "Ma'am, would you like me to have your food moved to another table? Our manager has agreed to comp your food due to the ... unfortunate circumstances."

Ana was cute, but too young for us and far too timid. She reminded me of a rabbit and that was definitely not what I wanted in my bedroom. The spicy omega, on the other hand, was more my speed. Despite having been closer to her, I had held my breath, and the other alpha's stench had prevented me from smelling her.

I needed to find an excuse to scent her soon to see if she might be a match for us.

"I'm so sorry, Ana," she apologized and placed a hand on the woman's arm. "He was so rude to you and I shouldn't have allowed it. Are you okay?"

"Me? Ma'am, you were the one who choked. If the alpha hadn't saved you ..." She stopped talking when she realized I was still there.

The omega I'd saved turned around and smiled. "Right, I'm so glad you were here or I might have died just now."

Her smile was like sunshine the day after sleeping in a trench in enemy territory. It warmed me and had me standing straighter.

Words were impossible as I stared at that smile.

"Please, come with me," Ana said and carried the plate away from the table and to a new table across the room, farther from us.

The omega's smile faltered as I stared at her silently, and she turned and hurried to follow the waitress.

"Kirk?" Buck asked as he came to my side.

"What was that?" the woman Tyler had brought to dine with us asked. "I can't believe an omega would dare to hurt an alpha. Why did you intervene?" She was barely thirty, a spoiled rich brat, and all she did was talk about herself and how awesome she was at being an influencer.

Undeserved rage at her questions filled me and I spun to glare down at her. "Why did I save her life? Are you suggesting I should have stayed to listen to you finish your insipid stories about manicures instead of preventing her from dying? How selfish are you?"

She stepped back, mouth agape at my anger, no words coming out of her mouth, despite it opening and closing several times.

"Yeah, this isn't going to work," Tyler said as he guided her away from us and up to the bar. "I'll buy you another drink as an apology for this not working out."

"You okay?" Buck asked the alpha who was just now getting to his feet.

"Fucking bitch," he whispered as he adjusted himself.

Buck stepped into my path before I could hit him,

guiding me back towards our table. "Come on, man. Let's go finish our drinks."

I growled at the pathetic man before us and begrudgingly followed Buck back to our table.

The omega I'd saved sat across the room eating her dinner, a sad look on her face as she finished eating alone.

"Doesn't she look familiar?" I asked softly.

"Yeah, but I can't place her," Buck admitted.

"Did you scent her?" I asked.

He shook his head. "I was more concerned with keeping you from killing that guy. What the heck was that, man? You want to get arrested while on vacation?"

I rubbed a hand down my face and shook my head. "I just reacted. Sorry."

He looked at the man who was now at the bar talking to the girl we'd rejected. "Yeah, I was about to hit him when the omega kicked him."

We both smiled at the memory.

"That was one hell of a kick," I said. "It's so rare to see an omega who stands up for themselves and others like that."

He nodded.

The omega stood, slung a beach bag over her shoulder, and walked out of the restaurant's back exit that led to the beach.

The pathetic alpha noticed, said bye to the girl at the bar, and followed after her.

I stood up immediately and followed them, ignoring Buck and Tyler's calls.

There was no way I was going to let him hurt her. Even if

she wasn't *my* omega, I wasn't going to let any alpha hurt an omega.

Never again.

"No killing!" Tyler yelled loud enough that I heard him as I walked out of the restaurant.

The sun was setting, and it turned the skyline into a brilliant, dark, fire orange color. I inhaled the salty ocean air, but it did nothing to relax me as I followed after the man who stalked after the omega.

Did she know he was following her?

What was he going to do?

I would grab him now, but I had to give him a chance to make a single move before that, so I could ensure I stayed clear with the law. Our pack did not need publicity while on vacation.

If Tyler's fans found out he was here, we'd be bombarded within the hour.

The omega wrapped her arms around herself as she walked to one of the private beaches, a scowl pulling her plump lips down. She was lost in thought and didn't notice the two alphas stalking her.

Once at the beach, she stopped, set her bag down, and removed her dress in a single motion.

I'd known her waist was small, but for some reason hadn't expected to find she had an hourglass figure beneath that dress.

Wide, luscious hips made her bikini bottoms ride up in the back, showing off a lot of pale, delicious skin, and a small black tattoo of a goose holding a knife in its beak.

The tattoo made me even more curious about her, but the more important thing was the alpha between us.

He seemed to have stilled once he saw her in her bikini, not that I could blame him, but now that she headed towards the ocean, he resumed stalking her.

His scent was so sour, full of bitterness and rage, that I had no doubt he was going to try something. I'd smelled similar scents on alphas when deployed, and they always attacked shortly after I scented them.

This time, I wouldn't let an omega get hurt before I intervened. I had to time it just right, so I subdued my scent, my alpha presence, and hid in the shadows, waiting for the perfect time to intercede.

CHAPTER 5
Brooklyn

THE WAVES CRASHED against the shore and the smell of salt was heavy on the breeze. The sun disappeared below the horizon and turned the sand orange for a brief moment as it set, like a silent explosion. The sand was cool and damp between my toes as I made my way towards the water.

Some were afraid of the ocean, the creatures within, but I knew this was their home. This was their territory, not mine, and I would respect them. I loved sharks and shark documentaries, so if I didn't flail too much while in the water or use boogie boards or surfboards, I felt like I was safe. Not that I'd been in the ocean much or seen a shark in person, but I had hope I wouldn't freak out.

The sun was bright enough that I could still see the wicker furniture adorned with brightly colored pillows and throws that lined the private beach. Only one other couple was still out there, their towels on the lounge chairs they had claimed, and their bodies in the surf as they splashed each other.

Tightening my hairband, I took a breath and walked into the water. It was so strange to walk into warm water. The lake at home in Tahoe was cold, being fed by the melting snow in the mountains. I *much* preferred this warm water to the icy lake.

Still, I shivered, though I wasn't certain why. Perhaps habit or a Pavlov reaction to touching water?

Walking until I was hip deep, I closed my eyes and spread my arms to my side.

The alpha who had saved me was ... odd. I'd barely gotten a hint of his scent, but he hadn't smelled bad at least. Although, the way he stared at me made me think that the scent appreciation was not mutual. I was thankful he had saved my life though, so I would find a way to repay him. Perhaps there was some way I could convince the hotel staff to let me pay for a night of their stay?

He was so large, and yet when he'd been performing the Heimlich on me, all I had felt was safety.

Was it a sign? Did it mean they were a possible match?

They had been chatting up that younger omega, though. She was likely more what they wanted. A quiet, docile omega who would do as they asked.

Most alphas I met didn't like an omega who spoke her mind, owned her own business, and did as she pleased.

I hadn't had the opportunity to fully scent him since I'd been choking to death, but I vowed to find the time to do so at my earliest opportunity.

That jerk who'd shared my table still pissed me off. I wished I was a big, strong alpha so I could beat him up nice and good. How dare he yell at Ana, who was just doing her job? How dare he get mad that the piece of fish I'd been choking on had landed in his beer! Like it was planned or anyone's fault!

If it weren't for the giant alpha, I would be dead right now.

"Hey, bitch!" the alpha from earlier yelled behind me. "Stay!"

I turned my top half, eyes wide in fear as he splashed into the ocean surf behind me. Out in the middle of the water, I had nothing I could use to save myself.

What could I do? Where could I go? How could I escape?

He had used an alpha command that my stupid, pathetic omega brain accepted and obeyed. So, I was currently at his mercy, my body refusing to move.

"You realize that you owe me an apology for humiliating me like that, don't you? Why don't you just open up that mouth and make up for the pain you made me—"

A huge, dark shadow fell over him from behind and in the next instant, he was lying in the surf, unconscious.

"Are you okay?" a deep, booming voice asked.

I recognized that voice. It was the one who had saved me.

Words wouldn't come out, my fear still raging through my system and making me stay rooted to the spot I stood.

He dragged the unconscious alpha who had come to confront me back to the beach, pulled a cell phone from his pocket, and called someone.

Sitting down, I let the warm water envelop me up to my shoulders.

Almost immediately, the large alpha was at my side, his large, warm hands cupping my face. "Are you okay?"

"Wh-Who are you?" I asked. "Did my dad send you to follow me?"

That would be my luck, someone I thought might be interested in me was actually a bodyguard Dad had sent after me. That had happened once before and had ended with an awkward conversation where I'd run off to cry alone in my room.

"My name is Kirk," he said. "I saw him following you and got worried, so I followed him, too. I'm sorry if I overstepped my boundaries, I don't know if he's part of your pack or—"

"I don't have a pack!" I shouted much too loudly. Exhaling harshly, I ran a hand down my face and shook it, trying to get rid of the heat in my cheeks as I backed up a little. "I'm sorry. So much has happened tonight. I, um, I just met that guy tonight and he was weird and then you stepped in and I, uh—"

He stepped closer to me, picked up my small hands in his giant ones, and rubbed his thumbs over the back of them. "It's okay. You're safe now. I won't let him hurt you."

His words eased my mind and I sagged forward, which allowed me to get his scent. A scent I recognized and made my eyelids flutter at its deliciousness.

Jerking my head up, my eyes widened as I looked at the mountain of a man. "Y-You!"

His brows furrowed. "What about me?"

"I ... I know you," I whispered.

"Kirk!" a male voice yelled.

The giant man released my hands and raised one of his arms. "Over here."

The two men from his pack rushed down the beach, stopping by the unconscious alpha.

"What happened?" the flirty one asked.

I stepped back from the giant man, Kirk, as recognition flooded through me. They were from my high school. The three before me had been one of the most popular packs, total bad boys who played pranks constantly, and every girl had tried to sleep with. Many claimed they'd been successful, but none had ever been confirmed.

Kirk frowned down at me. "It's okay, you don't have to be frightened of me."

"I have to go," I said, ran around him, between his two packmates, grabbed my bag, and fled back to the hotel.

There was no way they were without an omega. They'd had their pick of omegas in high school, and I doubted their adulthood had been any different.

No, I wouldn't be taken in by them. I refused to be toyed with by men bored on vacation, no matter how good they smelled.

Once back in my hotel room, I took a hot shower. The stress of the evening hit me and my knees gave out, forcing me to drop to my butt on the floor of the shower and let the water hit me.

Yet again, another alpha had come after me for retribution.

I really had to work on my mouth.

If Kirk hadn't been there ... I didn't even want to think about what could have happened.

Omegas were afforded more rights now, but still not the same as betas, let alone alphas. If an alpha attacked an omega, they questioned what the omega had done wrong before even thinking maybe the alpha was just an asshole.

It had taken video surveillance the last time I'd been attacked to convince the police that I had been fully the victim.

"Release the negativity and focus on the positivity," I told myself, eyes closed. "You're safe. You weren't hurt. You're alive."

Repeating it over and over to myself helped me relax, and after another twenty minutes, I climbed out of the shower and plopped into bed.

Kirk still smelled good, like redwood trees, but there was no way that he didn't have an omega of his own.

I wouldn't get my hopes up.

Plus, even if their pack was without an omega, it didn't mean I would smell good to them or that I was a fit for them.

Memories of the trio causing all kinds of problems in school returned and I rolled my eyes. Why did gorgeous males like them have to be such jerks?

They'd made my favorite English teacher, Mrs. Donovan cry. And they'd made my best friend, Alysse, cry when they harshly rejected her as a potential mate. And ... Tyler had made me cry and doubt myself.

Sure, it had been two decades since then, but did people really change that much?

I doubted it.

CHAPTER 6

Tyler

"LET ME GET THIS STRAIGHT," I said to Kirk as we sat in our hotel room after finding him with the omega he'd saved from choking at dinner. "You followed them and you thought the guy was going to assault her, so you knocked him out?"

He nodded.

"And she ran away from you, but you don't know why she ran?"

He nodded again.

I looked at Buck, eyes wide and brows raised. Was he any clearer on this than I was?

"I think she recognized me," Kirk added.

Now Buck's eyes were wide. "Wait, you know who she is?"

Kirk shook his head. "She smells familiar, but I still don't remember her. But she said she knew me."

"You didn't smell her?" I challenged.

"The ocean was too strong and I was too angry ..." He

dropped his head to look at his clenched fists. "That asshole distracted me."

Okay, for Kirk to be so distracted was an anomaly, which meant this girl was one we definitely needed to talk to and investigate.

"Did the cops give you a hard time?" Buck asked.

Kirk shook his head. "The hotel has surveillance cameras everywhere and were able to confirm my statement. They arrested the guy right away."

Well, that was a relief at least. Even if I didn't know the omega, I didn't want her to get hurt because of some asshole alpha on a power trip.

"So, I take it you want to talk to her again?" I asked.

He looked up, eyes wide, and nodded emphatically.

That ... was not the reaction I had expected.

"The concierge clerk let it slip that she's here for a week," I admitted to him. See, sometimes my flirting did come in handy. "So, we have time to talk to her."

"What if she leaves early because of all the problems?" Kirk asked, stood, and paced across the small living room of our suite.

"We can find out if she's going on any excursions and try to go with her," I suggested.

Kirk stopped pacing, stroked his jaw, and nodded. "Yes, yes. That's good. If we know her itinerary, we can keep an eye on her. Keep her safe."

I looked at Buck the same time he looked at me. Yeah, Kirk had it bad and hadn't even fully scented the omega. We definitely needed to do some searching and background investigation on her as soon as possible.

"I'll see what I can find out from the concierge clerk," I said quickly to calm him down.

He nodded and sat down in the chair, fingers steepled as he stared at nothing, lost in thought.

"I'm going to get us some drinks from the bar. I'll be right back," I said and stood.

Buck nodded once, knowing I was also going to do some recon without Kirk at my side. The big guy was one of my best friends, but the military had only increased his dominating aura, making others wary to talk in his presence.

Once outside of the room, I let out a breath and shook my head. Kirk had never reacted to a woman this way before. I needed to see if I could find her alone and talk to her. Although, after everything that had happened, I doubted she would be out and about on her own right now.

The bar was busy, but one dazzling smile at the young omega bartender and I was immediately being served.

I made sure to over tip her so I could follow up with questions later, if needed.

After getting the three drinks, I started to gather them to leave when I noticed the infamous omega at the other end of the bar, sitting alone and nursing what looked like a margarita.

Seizing the opportunity, I flagged the bartender back down, who rushed over eagerly. "What's she drinking?" I asked and tilted my head towards the omega.

She scowled. "The loner? She's drinking a margarita on the rocks."

I slid a ten-dollar bill across the bar and said, "Thanks."

Before she could respond, I carried my drinks over to the

seat beside the omega, growling softly to force the beta there to move. One thing I had discovered was that confidence was everything and even though I wasn't an alpha, I could act like one, and make even timid alphas do as I pleased.

Once seated, I turned and put on my charm as I smiled at the omega. "Hello."

She looked up, her eyes widened, and she leaned back slightly, putting more distance between us. "Um, hi."

It irked me that she was wary of me, but I didn't let it show. "You look really familiar, but I'm having a hard time placing you. Do we know each other?"

She flinched and spun the glass on the bar top as she stared at it. "Um, I think so."

When she didn't offer more, I asked, "Care to enlighten me?"

The sigh she released was so heavy I felt her breath across my arms. Her scent hit me like a sack of bricks and I shivered at the delicious aroma.

Holy gods of music, she smelled like freshly cut cedar, one of my favorite scents.

"Look, I don't mean to be rude, but I've had a really rough day and just wanted a drink to calm my nerves. Running into past acquaintances wasn't the plan, and won't help me relax. I don't mean to be rude and I'm sure tomorrow I'll be much more sociable, but tonight I will just say goodnight."

She stood, put a twenty-dollar bill on the counter, and threw back the rest of her drink in one chug.

My eyes fluttered closed as she walked by, her cedar scent wrapping around me like a warm hug.

A hug I remembered, but had tried my best to forget for decades.

"Brooklyn," I breathed, but when my eyes opened, it was too late, she was already gone.

I carried the drinks up to our room numbly, ignoring the eyes and blatant touches a few omegas gave as I made the journey.

Brooklyn. Brooklyn was here. Back in my life. Back in *our* lives.

"What took you so—" Buck stopped his question when he saw my face. "What happened?"

"I ran into her," I admitted, and passed out their drinks. Plopping down into my chair, I took a drink and closed my eyes.

"Her who?" Buck asked.

I opened my eyes and looked at Kirk. "Brooklyn."

He scowled, brain searching for the connection.

"Brooklyn?" Buck asked.

"High school," I added to jog their memories.

Buck's eyes widened. "No!"

I nodded. "Remember the little omega who yelled at us for the prank on Mrs. Donovan? The one Buck had asked about on the flight here?"

Kirk stood up suddenly, eyes bright. "Holy shit."

"That ... that was Brooklyn?" Buck asked.

I nodded. "She's definitely aged well and for some ungodly reason, she's still single."

"It's our second chance," Kirk said.

"What?" Buck and I asked simultaneously.

Had the big man finally lost his mind?

"I know you had a thing for her when we were sophomores," Kirk said to me.

My mouth set into a flat line and I refused to answer.

"And I know you were too immature to enjoy a feisty woman at the time," Kirk said to Buck.

Buck took a drink and stared at nothing, no response to Kirk given.

"She's the same age as us, single, and here. This has to be fate," Kirk said, excitement making him pace.

"We used up all our luck in our jobs," Buck whispered.

"Did we? Because I recall you being forced into an early retirement. I don't think that's luck," Kirk said.

"Kirk, what the fuck?" I yelled. How could he just say that to Buck knowing that it still haunted him?

Sure, Buck had been able to turn to coaching others after retiring, but it still haunted him that he'd been injured so severely, and didn't get to attain his dream of going to the finals.

"And my military career was far from rainbows," Kirk added. "I would gladly give up all that to have had her with me."

He looked at me and didn't speak, both of us knowing that there had been a lot of issues in my musical career, including having to forcibly remove women from my hotel rooms who tried to sleep with me, even after being turned down.

"We don't know anything about her," I countered. "We can't just take the circumstances as proof."

He rolled his eyes. "I know that, Ty. But we can't let this chance slip through our fingers, either."

"What do you propose?" Buck asked, still not looking at either of us.

"She's here for a week, just like us. Let's ask her out on separate dates and see if it progresses from there," Kirk suggested. "Buck should ask first."

Buck's head jerked up. "Me? Why me?"

"Because she's already wary of me and she just turned down Tyler."

I glared. "She didn't turn me down—"

"What do you say?" Kirk asked Buck, ignoring me.

"I'm not going to just run up to her," Buck grumbled. "But ... I'll see if there's an organic opportunity to approach her and ask her out."

"What's the worst that happens?" Kirk asked. "She can't be any worse of a date than the twerp we had with us tonight."

I ran a hand down my face and sighed. "She hadn't seemed so annoying when I first started talking to her."

Honestly, I should have asked her to leave much earlier in the night, but our prospects were so limited that I had given her as much of a chance as I could. Her getting mad that Kirk had saved Brooklyn was the nail in the coffin of the night.

"So, we are in agreement?" Kirk asked and looked between us both.

Being in agreement was vital to a pack, and I knew if I told him no that he would stop. No matter what heartbreak Brooklyn had put me through in high school, I couldn't let my inadequacies affect my brothers.

I nodded. "I'm in agreement."

"Me, too," Buck said.

Kirk smiled and I felt my chest tighten at the hopeful smile on the big lug's face. It had been so long since I'd seen such a genuine smile on him.

I hoped she didn't break us apart.

CHAPTER 7

Brooklyn

Ending up at the same place as my high school frenemies was not what I had expected for this trip.

Sure, the trio were great to look at, but in high school they'd caused me frustration after frustration. I'd even thought Tyler was a potential mate, until I caught him making out with my best friend, Alysse.

After that incident, I'd given up on them being suitors, and may have gone a little overboard on ruining any and all pranks and mischief they had planned.

Hopefully, I could enjoy my vacation even though they were here, but after being approached by Tyler last night, I didn't hold out much hope.

Maybe it was better to meet with them and turn them down right away, so they wouldn't try to pursue anything with me?

But ... what if ...

No, no there was no way that they were my mates. We would have figured that out in high school.

Right?

The warm sun was doing little to ease the flood of thoughts in my mind, so I decided to go for a swim.

As soon as I stood, I spotted one of the trio, already in the water.

Buck.

I knew he'd gone from our high school to a nice college, and had almost immediately been picked up to play on a professional football team. I also knew he suffered an awful injury that had forced him to retire early.

I hadn't wanted to keep tabs on him, but try as I might, I ended up stumbling upon articles about him. Although, I hadn't seen anything on him since his retirement, and none of the articles I'd read had shown his picture, which was why I hadn't immediately recognized him.

My inability to decide whether to run away or face him ended up giving him time to notice me.

He walked towards me, looking down slightly, and ran a hand through his wet hair as he approached. "Hello."

"Hello," I replied.

See, I was the queen of small talk. There was no reason I should still be single.

"I don't know if you remember me, or—"

"Of course I remember you, Buck," I interrupted him.

He raised his chin, meeting my eyes. "Are you okay? Kirk told us what happened with that asshat last night."

Fear flooded my system. I dropped my eyes to look at the water and took a few deep breaths, but it wasn't helping.

Buck reached a hand out towards me, but I took a step back and held my hand up.

"Just ... give me a moment."

His hand lowered.

After another few breaths, the fear finally subsided.

I looked up at him and gave a shaky smile. "Um, I'm fine. Sorry. These are things I'm working on with my therapist."

"Someone hurt you before?" he asked, his jaw tight and hands clenched into fists at his sides.

"Yes, but I'd rather not talk about that. I have to thank Kirk next time I see him. Speaking of that, how long are you guys here?"

If they were leaving soon, I could avoid them easily.

"A week," he answered.

Damn.

"So, what do you do for work?" he asked. "I don't know anything about you since high school."

"Well, you tend to lose touch with people when you go on to become a superstar," I teased.

He chuckled, and the tension finally left his body. He walked backwards and tilted his head towards the water. "We can swim and talk, if that's okay?"

My feet followed him, even though my words contradicted my movements. "You want to catch up with me? We weren't exactly friends in high school."

"You were a feisty handful," he said and smiled. "A frenemy."

"Frenemy, huh? I like the sound of that."

The water was warm, but still colder than the ambient temperature, so I shivered as I walked into the water up to my hips.

"So?" he prompted.

"I started my own business," I admitted. "It's doing pretty well."

"Your dads didn't take that too well, did they?" he guessed, mouth setting into a firm line.

Oh, right. They'd met my dads one time when the four of us were called to the principal's office, after I ruined one of their pranks. My dads had been furious and then when they found out it was a pack I'd gotten into it with, they'd been upset that I ruined a potential match.

"No, they did not like that I created my own business. Unfortunately for them, I did it all without their money, so they couldn't stop me."

"You didn't use their money?" he asked.

I shook my head and walked deeper, until the waves forced me to jump up when they came in. "I moved out when I turned eighteen and immediately found a job and started providing for myself. I still went back to visit them on occasion, but never accepted money from them even during the holidays. It drove them mad."

And why was I admitting so much to him? He didn't need all this backstory.

"Sorry," I apologized, "I ramble sometimes. Um, what about you? What'd you do after college? Where's your pack's omega?"

I was not going to admit that I knew about him.

"We don't have an omega," he answered immediately. "We haven't found her yet."

"Oh." Well, that was interesting.

"Did you find your pack yet?" he asked. His head was

turned away from me, but I had the feeling he was still looking at me, gauging my reaction and response.

Finally swimming past the waves, I floated on my back, closed my eyes, and answered, "No."

"Are you interested in finding a pack?"

It was a fair question. Not every omega wanted a pack.

"Yes." More than anything. "I've been searching. Even resorted to using agencies and allowed my mom to set up dates. So far none have worked out."

"Is that why you let that loser sit with you last night?"

I sat up, kicking my legs to tread water. "Yeah. He smelled awful, but I didn't want to be rude, either."

"I'm sorry you dealt with that. You could have asked us for help."

"You guys were with an omega and I hadn't completely recognized you yet." Something big swam beneath me and I squealed, immediately trying to swim towards the beach without making too many jerky motions while looking down at the water. I didn't want to flail and seem like an injured animal.

"What? What is it?" he asked, looking around. He spotted whatever it was and laughed.

"Why are you laughing?" I gasped as a wave splashed over my head.

Warm hands grabbed my waist and pulled me up against an even warmer body.

I wrapped my legs around his waist and wiped the water from my eyes. Normally, I didn't cling to men, but since he wasn't a complete stranger and I didn't want to drown or get eaten, I accepted the help.

He laughed as he walked us towards shallower water. "It was a sea turtle."

Heat bloomed along my cheeks and ears. "Oh." Realizing I was still wrapped around his body, I tried to push away. "I can walk. The one wave just caught me off guard."

"I think I saw a jellyfish," he said. "We should get out of the water."

"A jellyfish? There's no jellyfish here." Were there?

"Better safe than sorry," he said, and shrugged his large shoulders.

I looked around, but no one seemed to be paying any attention to us. When we got to my lounge chair, he set me down on it on my butt. "There, safe and sound back on land." He smiled down at me and it made me blush again.

"Thanks," I mumbled.

"Would you have lunch with me?" he asked. "I heard your stomach growling as we walked back."

There was no way he had heard my stomach growling, but I was hungry.

Should I eat with him?

"Well, seeing as you haven't told me about yourself yet, I suppose eating with you will give you the time to answer me. Can I change first?"

He stroked his chiseled jaw. "If I let you out of my sight, I'm worried you might run away."

"Run away? Why would I run away?" I asked.

"I seem to recall one of the last conversations we had, you said if you were my omega you'd find the first opportunity you could to run away and never look back."

He remembered that argument?

"I, uh, well ..." Instead of responding and embarrassing myself further, I dried myself off with my towel and slipped the new bathing suit cover on, which was basically just a moisture wicking dress.

His voice deepened as he bent closer to me and said, "You know, if you decided to run right now, I don't think I'd be able to stop myself from chasing you. The chase was always my favorite part, and you've always looked good walking away."

How had he known I was thinking about running away? I mean, not *actually* running, but fleeing. Despite my issues with other alphas, including the one from last night, his comment didn't scare me. Normally, it would have. Was it because I knew him already? I would have to discuss that with my therapist.

With his face so close to mine, I should have been able to smell him, but the stupid ocean breeze kept blowing it away. "Running isn't my forte," I said. "I'll just follow you to the restaurant. I doubt they'll throw me out for wearing this dress since it is a beach town."

"I'll make sure they don't throw you out," he promised and straightened.

Watching him walk to his lounge chair, I was afforded a nice view of his large, muscular back and round butt, and had to admit that he also looked good walking away.

Would those strong legs and butt provide for good ... thrusting?

I stood, trying not to laugh at my own stupid joke, but apparently my facial expressions still reacted.

"What's so funny?" Buck asked as he returned to me.

"Nothing. So, why aren't your pack mates with you? Did they abandon you to try to find omegas? Or did you all split up to try to cover more ground?"

My mouth just kept spitting out things I didn't want it to. It was definitely a condition.

Keeping stride at my side, he towered over me like a tree of muscle, blocking the sun from me as we walked. "They had some work to take care of, but they'll return soon. Would you like me to call them to join us for lunch?"

Would I? I still wasn't sure how I was going to react to speaking to Tyler. I'd seen him last night, but I had been so inebriated and tired that I just dismissed him and left.

"Um, actually I'd prefer to just have lunch with you. Is that okay?" Some packs wouldn't split up when courting, or potentially courting, an omega. I wasn't sure how their pack operated.

"That's fine," he said and gave me a warm smile. "It'll be nice to catch up with you by myself. It's rare that I have time alone anymore."

If I was there, he wouldn't be alone, but I kept that comment to myself.

A sudden gust of wind blew my hair across my face, forcing me to stop to try to smooth it back.

Buck's hands were suddenly there, assisting me. "Do you have a ponytail?" he asked.

Reaching deep within the beach bag, I managed to find the single ponytail that I had packed. I raised it up between two of my fingers with a triumphant smile. "I have one!" Taking my gathered hair out of his hands, I put it up in the ponytail and turned to face him. "Thanks for the assist."

He swallowed, his Adam's apple bobbed up and down, and nodded without speaking.

We finished our walk to the restaurant and were immediately seated. Buck pulled out my seat for me and pushed it in as I sat down.

The waiter brought out drinks for us while we looked at our menus to decide on food.

After deciding on my meal, I folded the menu and set it on the table. This gave me access to time to look at Buck.

His brows pulled down as he concentrated on the menu, deciding on his food. Age had done him well, he looked even more handsome now than he had in high school. He'd had a commanding presence in high school, yet had been quick to make people laugh and smile at games and parties. A few times, back when I thought they might be a potential match, he'd listened to me talk about issues I was having and helped me come to a decision. He had been a great listener, which had surprised me since he was so popular, unlike me.

"Are you ready to order?" the waiter asked, startling me.

"I'll have a chicken salad," I shouted and knew I had to be blushing.

"And I'll have a burger, medium, with fries," Buck ordered and handed the waiter our menus.

Trying to hide my embarrassment, I asked, "So, what have you been up to since college?"

"I played professional football for a bit, retired, and became a coach."

"Retired so early?" I asked, and tilted my head to the side.

"I got injured," he explained.

"I'm sorry."

"It's in the past and I've made my peace with it."

"What type of coaching do you do?"

"I do life coaching, inspirational speeches, and coach a few children's teams," he answered, smiling proudly.

"Sounds like a busy life," I commented. It didn't sound like he had much time for a mate.

"I've been slowing down recently. With my pack together and our hunt for an omega back on, I'm taking my time to focus on that instead."

Their hunt back on? Why had they stopped?

"You sure you should be spending your time with me, instead of out searching for an omega? You might have just abandoned her to that jellyfish."

He smiled and leaned forward. "I am searching for an omega currently."

I looked around the restaurant. "There aren't any single omegas in here except ..." Oh, he meant me! "I don't think I'm the omega you're looking for," I said sadly. "Wouldn't we have figured that out in high school?"

"I think we were all a bit too immature to properly decide," he countered. "If you aren't opposed to it, we would like to see if you are a match. I mean, what are the odds that after all these years we're reunited on vacation?"

That was true, but ...

"Did you ask Tyler about me? I'm pretty sure he made up his mind in high school." A wave of sadness hit me and I looked away from him to try to hide it.

"What do you mean?" he asked. "Did something happen between you two?"

Obviously, he hadn't told them about what had happened. "You should ask him."

The food came out, giving me a chance to avoid speaking more about it. Why hadn't Tyler told them what had happened? Why would he hide something from his pack? Maybe he hadn't thought it was necessary to tell them. That thought hurt even more.

Finished with my food, I grabbed some cash from my wallet, set it on the table, and stood. "Thank you for catching up with me. I hope you have a good rest of your day."

"Wait!" he barked, the order making me freeze as he reached across the table and grabbed my wrist. "Brooklyn, I don't want it to end like this. I can smell your pain. What's wrong?"

"It's an old wound that I hadn't realized still hurt, that's all. Don't worry, it'll pass soon." I smiled warmly at him and patted his arm. "Thank you for eating with me."

He reluctantly released me and sat down.

With his order over, I grabbed my bag and went to the clerk to schedule myself an excursion. Some time away from the resort and them sounded like a good idea.

CHAPTER 8
Buck

LETTING her leave had been hard, but I didn't want to force her to stay with me, despite wanting to ease the pain she felt.

Not after witnessing the brief bit of panic when I'd brought up the piece of shit from the previous night. Her reaction made me curious if there had been another alpha who had hurt her.

The most curious of all was her reaction to my question about Tyler.

Stalking through the hotel to get to our hotel room, everyone moved out of my way. No one wanted to get into the path of an angry alpha, but my size allowed my dominating presence to be even larger.

Two omegas stepped out of the elevator I waited for and immediately grabbed hands as they cringed and hurried away from me. Normally, that reaction would have hurt, but I was too frustrated to care at the moment.

"Hey, ass," I called out to Tyler when I entered the hotel room.

Kirk sat on the balcony, watching the people passing beneath, but quickly turned around with a quirked brow.

Tyler, blasting music from the television while writing something in one of his many journals, looked up. When he realized I was staring at him, he pointed at himself. "I'm an ass? What'd I do?"

"Yeah, that's exactly what I want to know. What did you do to Brooklyn in high school?" Getting closer to the beta was a bad idea, because – depending on his answer – I might punch him.

His brows rose almost to his hairline. "Uh, what do you mean? I didn't do anything to her. I never kissed her or anything."

Kirk marched into the living room, fists clenched, glare aimed at Tyler.

Tyler held his hands out towards each of us. "Easy, guys. It's not what you think. There's just been a misunderstanding."

"Explain," Kirk ordered him with an alpha bark that made even me flinch.

Tyler sighed and ran a hand down the back of his neck, looking off to the side, not at either of us. "I had a crush on her in high school, we'd been in band together and I wasn't the most confident when it came to her, but I did find times to interact. Don't misunderstand, I never fooled around with her, or even kissed her. We just hung out and acted like friends. We had almost gotten to the point where I was going to show her to you guys, to consider for courting, but then I found out she was going to that douche Tony's place after school and assumed she was doing it because she knew he was my nemesis. Then, she screamed at us for the Donovan prank. So, I may have ..." He paused, groaned, stood, and paced across the room. "... I made out with her best friend, making sure it was a spot she would catch us."

My eyes widened. "That's when she ramped up ruining our pranks and treating us like we were spoiled assholes."

"You made her think we didn't view her as a potential match," Kirk growled. "What the fuck, man?"

"I was stupid and immature, and my feelings were hurt because I thought she was leading me on! I've felt bad about it ever since I saw her reaction to finding us kissing that day, but I never had the courage to approach her, and then the three of us left." He plopped down onto the couch, leaned back, and closed his eyes. "I was cocky, and assumed that we'd find someone better and discredited her being a potential match."

"Why didn't you ever tell us?" I asked softly.

"You talked about her being a bitch all the time in high school. I figured I was right in assuming we weren't going to be a match."

"I called her a bitch because she kept fucking up our pranks and ruining our fun, because I didn't know you broke her heart!" I yelled. If I'd known, I never would have viewed her so negatively. Now, it made sense.

Tyler flinched.

"She still feels pain when she thinks about it," I growled at him. "You have to apologize."

"She wouldn't even talk to me last night. I doubt she's going to let me apologize now." His words were soft and sad. So, at least he was being honest about regretting it.

"I should punch you in the face," Kirk growled. "You might be the reason we've been single all this time."

"What do you think would have happened if we had discovered she was our match?" Tyler asked and opened his eyes to look at each of us. "Would you have passed on going pro? Would you have never joined the military? I sure as hell would have still gone on tour."

"You have to fix this," Kirk growled.

"We don't even know if she's a potential match still," Tyler argued and looked at me. "Do we?"

"She smells fucking delicious," I said, recalling her cinnamon scent. "It was muted because of the ocean water and wind, but one whiff had me frozen in place." I looked over at the tense Kirk. "And he's acting far more concerned with her emotional and physical safety than he would for others."

"I'll try to talk to her and scent her," Tyler agreed. "The easiest way would be finding out if she's going on any excursions and tagging along with her." He stood and stretched. "I'll go flirt with the clerk and see what I can get out of her."

"Make sure Brooklyn doesn't catch you flirting," Kirk said, spun, and stormed back to the balcony.

Tyler grumbled beneath his breath as he headed to his room to get changed.

Sensing Kirk's irritation, and knowing he likely wanted to find out what I'd talked to her about, I made my way to the balcony and sat in the chair next to him.

We sat in silence, watching the other guests playing in the ocean, sunbathing, or out for a walk.

As soon as we heard the hotel door open and shut with Tyler's departure, Kirk simply said one word, "Spill."

I laughed and shook my head. "Sometimes you are so predictable, man. There's nothing much to spill. She has her own business, and is still searching for a pack. She said she even used some agencies. Also, she's been hurt by someone before, but she didn't want to talk about it. She had a brief panic attack when I mentioned it."

"Someone's hurt her before? That's probably why she fled when that ass followed her and I stopped him." His hands fisted until his knuckles were white. "How fucked up is it that we might've missed out on our omega, all because of teenage jealousy?"

"I'm not positive she's our match, but she does smell good, and it felt easy to be around her when I ate lunch with her."

"You ate lunch with her?" Kirk asked and sat up a little, eyes wide. "Why didn't you call us down?"

"She asked to eat with just me. I think because of Tyler. She didn't say she wouldn't consider us for courting, but did say I needed to ask Tyler first. Because of his stunt, she thinks he didn't want her."

"I'm going to punch him so fucking hard," Kirk growled.

"We've got to play this right. We can't fuck it up again," I whispered. "I'm too old for this shit, and just want to settle down and have kids."

Whether that was with Brooklyn or not was undecided, but I wanted to see this through to be one hundred percent certain.

"It's going to be hard with her being more afraid of alphas," Kirk said.

I looked at the big man and understood his hesitation. His size and almost permanent scowl had a lot of people hesitant to interact with him. Due to this, he was a chatterbox, to put people at ease.

"I don't think it'll be as hard as you think," I argued. "She said next time she saw you, she was going to thank you for protecting her."

His eyes widened. "She did?"

I nodded. "Just be your normal chatty Cathy and it'll be fine."

We sat in contemplative silence for several minutes, both of us likely thinking about Brooklyn.

"Is he right?" he asked.

"You're going to have to be more specific," I replied, rolling my head to look at him.

"I know you two wouldn't have given up on your dreams, even if we had found her. What would have happened to us if we had realized she was our omega back then? Do you think we might have never found our opportunities, or might have never split up? Would she have kept us together?"

"There's no use worrying about what could have been. We just have to do our best to ensure a better future."

He growled softly and nodded. "Right."

"Also, she's still feisty. I accidentally barked at her, and although she obeyed, she was irritated about it. I think with a little coaxing, we can bring back the little spitfire to full aggression." And once she was back to full spunk, I would have a lot of fun with her in and out of the bedroom.

CHAPTER 9

Brooklyn

FOR HALF AN HOUR, I stood at the desk looking over the different excursions, trying to decide which to go on.

Two omegas walked up behind me, whispering about a scary alpha.

I turned to ask what alpha, but realized I knew them. "Stacy? Alexa?"

Their eyes widened and they hugged me. "Brooklyn!" they both squealed.

We had all worked together at a restaurant as waitresses when I was eighteen.

"What are you doing here?" Stacy asked. Her long, dirty blonde hair was up in a ponytail and her green eyes shone with excitement.

"I'm on vacation," I explained.

"With your pack?" Alexa, tall and thin, with dark brown hair, looked like a model.

"No," I admitted, "I still haven't found mine."

"Neither have we!" they shouted simultaneously.

"Are you guys planning an excursion for tomorrow?" I asked. "We should all go together!"

"Yes! Let's go together!" Stacy agreed, nodding her head emphatically.

"I've been here half an hour, and can't make up my mind," I admitted. "So, I'll go with whatever you guys choose."

"Which ones were you deciding between?" Alexa asked and leaned forward to look at the options.

"Sea turtle snorkeling, cruise to the sunken volcano, or the jungle ziplining," I answered and pointed at each in turn.

"The ocean scares me," Stacy admitted. "So, I'd like to avoid snorkeling."

"The ziplining sounds like a lot of fun," Alexa said.

"I'm up for ziplining. Stace?"

She nodded. "Ziplining it is!"

The petite omega in front of us smiled, but it was definitely forced as she said, "I'm glad you were able to help her make a decision."

It's not like I'd been pestering her or asking tons of questions. Why was she so irritated with me?

"There will be a truck to pick you up and drive you up into the mountainous jungle for ziplining tomorrow morning at eight a.m. You just go to the valet to check in. Make sure you wear comfortable closed toe shoes, and put some bug spray on. The jungle has lots of mosquitos. I'd also recommend pants and a long sleeve shirt, but that's up to you guys. It just helps prevent bug bites. I'll just need you to sign these forms and you'll be all set to go since you get one excursion for free."

We took the forms and offered pens over to a group of chairs around a coffee table to fill out the papers. They were average consent forms for pictures and waivers in case of injury.

"I can't believe we met up at a place like this," Stacy said as she filled out her papers. "What's it been, ten years?"

"Twenty," I admitted with a cringe.

"Oh, man. We are getting so old," Alexa mumbled. "I did not expect to be single at forty."

"Same," Stacy and I said simultaneously.

We all laughed and resumed filling out our paperwork.

Once done, we turned everything in and then decided to catch up over drinks.

"To the bar!" I shouted, more than excited to have a drink after the emotional meeting with Buck.

"Hello, beautiful," Tyler said behind me.

I turned around, expecting him to be talking to me, but he was talking to the omega at the excursion desk.

"H-Hi," she stammered and blushed.

"I have a small favor to ask," he requested and gave her puppy dog eyes.

"Come on, let's go get that drink," I whispered, and pushed Stacy and Alexa towards the backdoor that led to a tropical themed bar.

The last thing I wanted was to watch him flirt with another woman.

"You know him?" Alexa whispered and looked over her shoulder. "Oops, he noticed you leaving."

"Knew him in high school," I admitted. "Don't want to talk about it."

Stacy looped her arm through mine. "We definitely need that drink."

Once at the bar, we opted to sit at the bar top instead of at a table. Stacy and Alexa sat on either side of me, which I appreciated, because it prevented anyone else from sitting next to me.

The bartender, a sexy beta with dimples and washboard abs on display hurried over to us. "What can I get you beautiful ladies?"

"Lemon drop," I ordered.

"Mai Tai," Alexa ordered.

"Do you have anything that tastes like strawberries?" Stacy asked, leaning her chin on her elbows that were propped up on the top, allowing her cleavage to be on full display.

"I've got the perfect strawberry drink for you," he said, and winked.

Stacy turned towards me and said, "Okay, update us on what's happened in the last twenty years. You just disappeared from the restaurant one day."

I did not want to be a downer, so I only told them the positive things that happened, mainly my business.

"That's amazing that you started your own business," Alexa cheered. "I'm super jealous. I'm still working as a waitress and hating people more and more each day."

"Retail and customer service jobs definitely bring out the negative side of humans," Stacy agreed.

"What about you, Stace?" I asked, smiling at the bartender when he put my drink down in front of me.

"I'm working as a secretary, and it's actually really fun.

I'm in charge of the CEO's calendar, trips, proofreading letters, and scheduling meetings. I thought it would be super boring, but it's actually entertaining." She brightened as she talked about it, and I couldn't help but return her smile, glad she'd found something she enjoyed.

"That's awesome!"

Out of the corner of my eye, I saw Tyler enter the bar area and tensed, but he veered out of my line of sight, behind me.

"He's following you," Stacy said in a whisper around her straw as she took a drink.

"Where?" I asked without turning my attention away from her.

"A table just a little back. If we talk at a normal volume, he'll definitely hear," she whispered.

Wonderful.

"So, neither of you found your pack yet either?" I asked, returning to a regular volume.

"No," Alexa said with a sigh. "I've gone to several agencies, too, but at this point I'm feeling like an old maid."

"Pretty sure we're all dealing with midlife crises," Stacy said. "At least that's what my family keeps telling me."

I scoffed. "Mine, too."

"I met one pack that I thought was going to work, they all smelled okay and we got along, but then another omega showed up, and they were like moths drawn to a flame. I guess her scent was better than mine." Alexa's pain was evident, and Stacy and I both instinctually reached out and set a hand on her shoulders.

She smiled. "It's okay, it was several years ago."

"Yeah, but things that happened a long time ago still hurt," I acknowledged, and then immediately cringed when I remembered that Tyler was nearby. "My therapist said that as long as you acknowledge the pain, why you feel it, and accept it, that you're well on your way to moving on."

"It'd be easier to move on if I had delicious men in my bed," Alexa said.

Stacy and I laughed.

"How are you guys dealing with heats?" Stacy asked.

"Clinics," Alexa answered with a cringe. "I hate them, but since I live in a big city, it's my only option."

"I use them, too," Stacy said. "And take tranquilizers to dull the pain and insanity."

"I'm able to use the shed my dads built for me on their property still," I admitted, feeling like a spoiled rich bitch saying it. "I did use a clinic a couple of times, but hated it. I've also taken the tranquilizers, but hate how they make me feel."

"I started using suppressants, but the side effects are awful," Alexa said.

"Same," Stacy said with a nod.

I hadn't resorted to using suppressants, but had considered it when I started my business.

"My mom said she took them before she found her pack and warned me against them," I commented.

"How is your mom doing? I saw on the news that you lost three of your dads. I'm so sorry about that." Alexa set a hand on my forearm.

"She's doing a lot better now. It was touch and go for a bit after they died, but my remaining dad really stepped up to take care of her needs. I think that extra burden is why he's pushing me so hard lately to pack up."

"Our parents just want us happy and they know we aren't," Stacy said. "It's hard on alphas when they see omegas unhappy, even ones that aren't theirs. My dads are the same way."

Alexa nodded. "Mine started sending me on blind dates and paying for them."

"Maybe we're just destined to be without a pack," Stacy said. "I'd take a single alpha at this point."

Alexa and I nodded our agreement.

"One alpha is better than alone," I added.

"Maybe our packs are just in other states," Alexa suggested. "I have heard of omegas finding their packs in their forties."

"Fingers crossed," Stacy said, causing us all to laugh.

"I'm going to try to travel more," I said. "Maybe I'll visit all fifty states, or at least as many as necessary until I find my pack."

"What if we travel together?" Alexa suggested. "It would be safer. You guys heard about the kidnapped omegas, right?"

I cringed and took a drink before nodding. "Yeah, the ones that they used for breeding."

"It's so awful," Stacy whispered. "I can't imagine how terrified they were, and how much therapy they're going to have to go through after that. And they didn't even catch the ringleader of the whole operation, so he could still be out there."

"What kidnappings are you talking about?" Tyler asked behind me.

"It was all over the news," Stacy said. "There is a ring of alphas stealing single omegas and keeping them in hidden areas, impregnating them when they're in heat, and then selling the babies to couples that can't have them."

"Where was this?" Tyler asked, stepping closer to my back, so close I could feel his warmth radiating off of him.

"Um, Tyler, this is Stacy and this is Alexa," I introduced, feeling obligated. "They're both omegas I met at my first job. Stacy and Alexa, this is Tyler. His pack is here, searching for an omega."

Why did I introduce him that way? It was like I wanted them to see if they were matches with them.

"I'm sorry to interrupt," Tyler said. "I just wanted to find out more about what you were talking about. That's absolutely awful and terrifying."

"It happened in a nearby state, but I can't remember which one," Stacy answered.

"Tyler," Kirk called out somewhere near the entrance, but I didn't turn to face him.

"It was nice to meet you two. Brooklyn, I'd like to talk to you tomorrow, if that's okay?" His voice softened when he asked me.

"Um, okay," I agreed, uncertain how to respond.

Stacy made a kissy face at me where he couldn't see and got a scowl from me in return.

"Bye," Tyler said.

Once he was gone, Stacy and Alexa turned to me with wide eyes.

"Okay, what the hell is up with you two?" Stacy demanded. "You obviously have a past."

I sighed. "We knew each other in high school. I'd thought we might be a match, but before I really had a chance to find out, I caught him making out with my best friend."

"So, he was trying to make you jealous to see your reaction?" Alexa asked.

I opened my mouth and immediately closed it. "I, uh, never thought about that being a possibility. I just assumed he was showing me that he didn't view me as a match."

"Men are weird," Stacy grumbled. "I can't say for sure what he was doing, but that man was definitely interested in you."

"He was just flirting with the excursion receptionist," I argued. "That's why I pushed you guys out."

"Again, maybe he's trying to gauge your reaction to see if you're jealous. Were you jealous?" Alexa leaned forward, a wicked smile on her face.

"Bartender! Another round, please!" I yelled instead of answering her.

Alexa and Stacy burst into laughter, my reaction obviously what they had expected.

"So glad I can make you laugh after all these years," I teased.

That made them laugh until tears leaked from their eyes.

CHAPTER 10

Brooklyn

CHUGGING an energy drink after downing some medicine for headaches was definitely helping the hangover I had, but not as much as I would have liked.

Especially since I'd had to wake up early to go ziplining.

"Brooklyn?" Kirk asked.

I turned and smiled up at him. "Hello, Kirk. I was hoping to see you. I wanted to say thank you for saving me the other day. I realized that I hadn't thanked you."

We stood in the middle of the hallway near the elevators. I'd come down here to use the restroom before we left, since I wasn't sure how long the drive would take, and I hadn't thought to do it while in my hotel room.

"Are you going ziplining, too?" he asked.

I froze at his question and looked at his long sleeve shirt, khaki shorts, and boots, realizing he was definitely dressed for the jungle. "Wait, you guys are coming, too?"

He frowned. "Yeah, is that a problem?"

"I, um, well, I was hoping to spend the day with my friends."

He smiled. "I thought we were friends?"

Right. I was being a total jerk right now.

"Of course, I'm glad we'll have you guys with us." I gave him my warmest smile.

He stepped closer to me, opened his mouth, but froze, his eyes widening a bit in what appeared to be shock.

"Kirk?" I asked, and closed the final step separating us. "Are you okay?" As soon as I asked, his scent filled my nostrils, the forest in summer with the sunlight shining warmly on my skin. My body moved on its own, forcing me forward to press my nose into his chest to inhale more of his scent. I had never smelled a man this delicious before. I knew he smelled like the forest, but there was something about it now, it was so strong, so wonderful.

"Brooklyn? Where are you?" Alexa called. "The truck is here."

Her voice snapped me out of my trance and I jerked back from Kirk, my face burning in embarrassment. "I, uh, sorry, I, um." A full sentence was trying to form, but my brain and mouth weren't aligning. So, instead of embarrassing myself further, I spun and ran towards the entrance.

"Stop!" Kirk barked.

The order forced me to stop midstride. I hated alpha orders and my stupid omega brain that obeyed them.

Listen, brain, we obeyed the order and stopped, so now we can move again. Go!

I took two more steps before Kirk barked the order again, forcing me to stop again. After a breath, I moved again.

He growled as he neared me, but I didn't dare look back to see how close he was. It was only a few more feet to the doors.

Exhaling harshly to expel the last of his scent from my nostrils, I ran as fast as I could out to the valet area where Stacy and Alexa waited.

"There you are," Stacy said with a smile. Her smile shrank when she realized I was panting. "What's wrong?"

"Nothing, just took the stairs and I'm out of shape," I lied and rubbed my face.

"Your truck is right over here," a tall man wearing camouflage pants and shirt said. He had a thick beard covering half of his face and a hat that only allowed us to see his eyes. The truck he indicated was a Jeep, just big enough for the four of us to fit.

"Morning ladies," Tyler greeted off to my right. "You guys ready for a fun day of ziplining?"

"Ah, you three will be in the second truck," camouflage man said, and pointed at a second Jeep with a man standing beside it. The man raised his hand and waved with a smile. He also wore camouflage, but no hat.

"We're taking separate trucks up?" Kirk asked, the unease obvious in his voice.

"Come on," I said, grabbed Stacy and Alexa by the hands, and dragged them to the first Jeep. Stacy took the front passenger's seat, while Alexa and I climbed in the back.

Camouflage man climbed in the driver's seat, took off his hat, and smiled warmly at us. "Buckle up. The highways are smooth, but the road we have to take to get to the ziplining area is a bit bumpy. Oh, and I'm John. I'll be helping you all today, ensuring you arrive safely and have a fun time."

"We're looking forward to it," Stacy said.

Chancing a glance back, I saw Kirk arguing with the second driver as they got into the other truck.

"Let's go!" John said, turned on dance music, and drove away, leaving the trio behind. "So, where are you ladies from?" he asked.

Instead of engaging with him in conversation, I let Stacy take the helm on that. I spent the drive looking at the beautiful scenery and trying to rationalize why Kirk had smelled so good.

Had my nose been off? Maybe I was sick and that had tricked my senses? Yes, that had to be it. It didn't make any sense for one person to smell so much better than others.

And yet ... I had heard from my sisters that this was how they felt their husbands smelled.

But the look on Kirk's face when I'd been close to him was not a happy one. Had I smelled bad to him? Was it possible for us to have drastically different opinions on the other's scent?

Had I smelled so bad that he'd been speechless? But then why had he tried to order me to stop? I shouldn't have run from him, but I had never in my life thrust my face into a man's chest to smell him like that.

"You okay?" Alexa asked me.

I nodded. "Just enjoying the beautiful scenery."

"It is gorgeous, isn't it?" she agreed with a smile.

"It's going to look even better when you are sailing through it on the zipline," John said. "The route it takes is truly breathtaking. Prepare yourselves, ladies. We are going off road now!" He turned onto a dirt path that hardly looked like a road or even a path, but there were obvious signs of others having used the path, such as tire tracks.

He hadn't been lying about it being rough. He had to slow down several times as we drove over large bumps in the road and through some muddy holes.

I gripped the door handle tightly, breathing through my nose to try to calm down. I knew we would be going into the jungle for this excursion, but it felt like he was driving us into the middle of nowhere. We drove down the dirt path for over thirty minutes. A glance at my phone confirmed that there was no cell reception up here, either.

It made sense why they wanted us to go so early in the morning. I did not want to be out here in the middle of the night.

"Almost there," John said. "Because the jungle is protected, we aren't allowed the pave the road here. We asked about just bringing in equipment to level the road out, and that was denied as well."

"It's understandable that they'd want to protect the jungle. We've lost a lot of forests and jungles over the past fifty years," Stacy said.

"And a lot of the animals that inhabit this area are endangered," John added with an agreeing nod. "That's why hunting here is strictly forbidden."

We approached a huge, red, wooden barn that had a couple other Jeeps parked next to it. A few men walked around wearing camouflage or khaki pants.

Were they company issued? Did they force them to wear them as a dress code?

"Alright, let's get you ladies geared up," John said as he parked and climbed out.

We climbed out and followed after him towards the barn. Looking around, I didn't see any ziplines. Were they on the other side of the barn? The forest didn't look clear enough here.

"Something about this place feels wrong," Alexa whispered to me, walking so close our arms touched constantly.

I nodded. "It doesn't look like there's a zipline here."

Stacy came up to our side and asked, "Is it just me, or are all these guys looking at us strangely?"

Now that she mentioned it, I looked around at the men there and had to agree. They were looking at us almost hungrily. Plus, there wasn't a single woman anywhere in sight.

"Maybe we should wait for the second truck," I suggested. "My friends shouldn't be too far behind us."

John realized we'd slowed down and turned around. "Come on, ladies! The sooner you get geared up, the sooner you can get on the ziplines!"

"We want to wait for our friends," I said, and gave him what I hoped was a charming smile.

"They'll be right behind you," he said. "Plus, it's going to take a little bit to get all the safety gear on."

I knew we had to get into harnesses and put on helmets, but did it really take that long?

"Let's just go," Alexa whispered. "I don't want to stand out here with all these men staring at us."

"Okay," I agreed, giving one last look behind us at the road we'd taken to get here, but the other Jeep still hadn't arrived. They hadn't been that far behind us, had they?

John opened a small door on the side of the barn and waved us in with a smile.

The three of us stepped inside and found three men with harnesses in their hands and helmets next to their feet. The barn had no windows, just a few lights along the roof, which made for really eerie lighting. The men waited for us with kind smiles.

Maybe we were just being paranoid, after all.

The men helped us into the harnesses and gave us yellow helmets, before leaving us alone with John.

"Alright, let's go over the rules," he said as he walked towards a door on the far side.

We followed him, still staying close together. Even though they had geared us up, something still felt off.

And where the hell were Kirk, Tyler, and Buck?

"You'll have two clips," John explained, "and you'll always have one secured. So, if you move from one line to the next, make sure you keep one on the current line, while you move the second to the next line, then remove the first clip and move to the second line. Does that make sense?"

"Yes," we answered.

"Never reach up and grab the lines with your hands. You'll tear them up," he said as he pushed open the door and waved us inside.

We stepped into the room, but it was pitch black.

"Um, I can't see a thing," Stacy said.

"The final rule is do not, under any circumstances, run,"

John said, and closed the door, enveloping us in complete darkness.

"Run?" Alexa asked.

I reached out my hands in the dark at my sides, trying to find Alexa and Stacy.

A blindingly bright light turned on overhead, making me flinch and turn my face down to give my eyes time to adjust.

The three men who'd helped us into our harnesses walked towards us with syringes and ropes in their hands.

I looked around and realized my gut had been right. Something was wrong. There were no windows in this room, and the only other door was blocked by a huge man with a gun on his right hip and a knife on his left side.

"Wh-What are you doing?" Stacy asked and backed up a step.

"Sorry, but ziplining has been cancelled," one of the men in front of us said with a sneer.

No. No way. This couldn't be happening.

I grabbed Stacy's and Alexa's hands and said, "We've got to get out of here."

"There's f-four of them," Stacy pointed out.

"Just follow my lead, okay?" I whispered.

Following the side of the wall, I headed towards the giant man.

"You guys really don't want us. We're old and likely infertile by now," I said.

"S-Super infertile," Stacy agreed.

Alexa nodded emphatically with eyes wide as saucers.

"We'll be the judges of that," one of the men said as they

followed us in slow, unhurried steps. "This will help us find out really quick," he said and held up the syringe.

"You aren't going to get away with this," I said. "My f-friends will come for us."

"Your friends are on the other side of the jungle, likely already ziplining and having a grand time. There's no one who knows about this spot, and no way you can escape or find your way back. Don't worry, we'll keep you fed and healthy."

The three men darted forward, injected us each with the syringes, and stepped back with creepy smiles.

I pressed a hand to my arm where I'd been injected. "Wh-What was that?"

"It helps us find out who's fertile and who isn't," the big man, who was now behind me, said.

I spun around and kicked him as hard as I could in the junk.

The guy fell to his knees, clutching himself.

I grabbed the gun from the holster and pointed it at the back of his head.

Everyone in the room stopped. I was pretty sure no one was even breathing.

"Open the door," I ordered Stacy.

Alexa threw it open and stepped out first. Stacy followed her.

"If you run, you'll just get punished when we do catch you," one of the men growled.

"If you chase us, I'll shoot you in the dick," I threatened. "So, just let us go."

Talking was pointless, plus there were guys outside, so we needed to run as fast as we could.

I smacked the big guy in the back of the head with the butt of the gun and ran out the door without looking back.

The girls looked at me with wide eyes, trembling as they stood facing two large men.

My dads had trained me to use guns from the time I was ten years old. I didn't enjoy them and never owned one personally, but I still knew how to use one.

"Just put the gun down," one of the guys ordered me.

"Stacy. Alexa. We have to run. Run into the woods back towards the road, but don't run down the path we took to get here exactly, okay?"

They nodded, not speaking.

"Ready? Run!" I squeezed the trigger twice, shooting each man once in a leg.

Stacy and Alexa immediately started running towards the tree line, back towards the highway.

"Stop!" an alpha barked.

The three of us halted.

I turned, raised the gun, and shot at the alpha, but missed.

He yelped as he dove away.

"Run!" I ordered the girls who sprang into action again.

"This is crazy!" Alexa screamed as we ran.

"Don't stop! Just run! If they order you to stop again, pause and then go again. Remind your brain you only have to follow their order for a second," I yelled as we ran.

The forest was dense, but thankfully the underbrush was

pretty clear, so we could run without too much worry of tripping.

"Where'd you learn to shoot like that?" Alexa asked.

"My dads. We lived in the forest, and there were bears, so they wanted me to know how to shoot in case I encountered one. I hate guns."

"I love them right now, and you," Stacy said.

"Come back!" someone yelled, but thankfully it wasn't a bark, so we just ignored them.

"Are we headed in the right direction?" Stacy asked.

"I think so," I replied and panted. "Away from them is the best option, even if it isn't in the exact right direction."

"This was not the relaxing vacation I had envisioned!" Alexa growled.

"Well, I always said I wanted to work out while on vacation," I said, to try to lighten the mood. "I'm definitely getting a workout from this run."

"Your jokes have always sucked!" Stacy said.

I huffed a laugh, but decided not talking was probably a good idea. "Let's try to be quiet here on out to lose them."

The two nodded their agreement.

Stacy slipped on some leaves and Alexa grabbed her arm, righting her so she didn't fall.

We ran through a swarm of bugs that made Alexa screech and swat at them.

A fallen tree loomed ahead, so we veered right around it, but stopped on the other side to catch our breath.

"I can't keep running," Stacy gasped, sucking in air.

"We just need to keep moving. Walking is good."

"Does anyone have cell reception?" Alexa asked as she pulled out her cell phone and held it up.

"Nope," I replied.

I wished I had gotten at least one of the trio's numbers, so I could have sent a text or SOS to them just in case we did get reception somewhere.

We removed the helmets and set them on the ground. The bright yellow color would definitely give us away if we kept wearing them.

After drinking some of the water each of us brought, we started walking.

It worried me that we didn't hear the guys behind us, but I wasn't going to look a gift horse in the mouth.

We walked in silence for a long time. The area was full of foliage, and we had to be careful where we stepped. Several times one of us slipped, and we constantly smacked at bugs trying to bite us, even with bug spray on.

"Do you think they gave up?" Stacy asked in a whisper the next time we stopped for a break.

We sat down and drank more of our water. Alexa had been smart enough to bring some granola bars, so we shared one, trying to ration it just in case we were out here longer than a few hours.

"I doubt it," I said, and swallowed hard. "Maybe they just can't track worth shit."

"Maybe they got scared, because they haven't encountered an omega who can shoot before," Alexa suggested with a smile for me.

The three of us laughed.

"You think the hotel will give us a refund, since this excursion turned out so bad?" I asked.

"I hope your friends are okay," Stacy said. "You think they took them to the actual ziplining place?"

"I'm sure they're fine," I said, though truthfully, I was a little worried about them too.

Alexa rubbed at her arm where they'd injected her. "What do you think they injected us with?"

"I don't know, but I don't feel any different right now," I said, frowning as I tried to figure out what it could be. I wasn't sleepy or woozy, so it wasn't a sedative.

He had mentioned finding out if we were fertile. Was this some type of fertility drug? That made no sense, though. There weren't drugs like that. Were there?

"Let's keep moving," Stacy said, and stood. "We need to reach some type of civilization in order to be saved. These bugs are out for our blood, just as much as those assholes."

We resumed walking and a rush of warmth flooded me, making me stumble.

Was that a heat flash? No, it was too soon for my heat.

I fanned my face and kept walking. I was likely just fatigued from the sweltering heat of the jungle and the fear that still coursed through me. The highway couldn't be too far away, so we just had to keep walking.

CHAPTER 11

Buck

Kirk fisted his hands in the shirt of the driver and slammed the smaller man into the wall. "Tell me where they took them!" The bark was so intense that it made both Tyler and I flinch back a step.

"I-I don't know what you're talking about," he said, eyes wide and panicked.

"The cops don't go lighter on accomplices," I said. "So, the sooner you give them up, the better."

Kirk growled, and the man swallowed hard.

"They take the omegas to a different place. I don't know where. I was paid to drive you guys to the zipline place and take you ziplining. That's all I know. I swear!"

"There's no cell service out here," Tyler advised us. "We can't call the cops from here. We'll have to go back towards town."

"No, there has to be a landline here, or a satellite phone. They wouldn't be without some form of communication device on the chance that someone gets hurt and they have to call an ambulance," Kirk argued. "Where is it?"

"Th-There's a landline in the office," the man said, and raised a shaking hand to point towards the small building across the parking lot.

"I'll go call while Kirk ties this guy up," I said, and jogged across the parking lot to the office.

After explaining the situation to the emergency dispatcher, I agreed to wait for the cops before we left.

Kirk didn't like that at all. "We have to go find her. They could be anywhere in the jungle, and who knows what ..."

I set my hand on his shoulder. "We have to wait for the cops. They know this area better than us. It won't do her any good if we just run off into the jungle and get lost ourselves."

He growled, but nodded.

The driver sat tied up in the office chair, shaking.

"Do you think this has to do with the kidnappings they told me about yesterday?" Tyler asked as he paced across the office.

I growled. "Let's hope not."

"If they lay one finger on her, I'll murder every single one of them," Kirk snarled.

"Three omegas against one alpha aren't terrible odds," I said, trying to give him some hope, despite feeling none myself.

"He likely took them somewhere with backup," Kirk said, and shook his head. "She may fight our barks, but she's not immune to them."

The cops pulled up and we spent the next ten minutes

giving them our statements and providing as much information as we could. It helped that Kirk was so observant and had memorized the license plate. The driver told them the same thing he told us and they immediately put him in handcuffs and drove him to the station.

"We put out a call on the plate, and we'll search some of the areas we know about, but there's a lot of jungle and a lot of paths locals take that aren't marked. The best thing you can do is go back to the hotel and wait for us to contact you with more information."

We waited until the last cop left before facing each other.

"What's the plan, Kirk?" I knew him, and he was not going to go back to the hotel and just wait.

"We take the Jeep and search for paths on our own. More of us searching means more chances to find them," he said.

Tyler nodded. "And hopefully find them faster. I don't want to think about what might happen if they're left in the jungle after dark."

"We don't have the keys, though. They're probably still on the driver they just took in," I pointed out.

Kirk held up his closed fist, opened it, and let the keys dangle before us. "I pocketed them before the cops came."

Of course he had.

"Do you have an idea of which way to start?" I asked.

Kirk nodded and pulled out his phone, going to the map app. We didn't have cell service, so it couldn't pull up our location, but he used his fingers to scroll the map to where the hotel was. "We followed them down this highway." He moved the map along the route. "I thought I saw them continue this way, while we veered off here, but they were too far ahead for me to be certain it was them."

There were a lot of similar Jeeps driving around, which was likely part of their plan.

"I say we go back to this point and continue on."

"Sounds like a plan to me," Tyler said, and headed out of the office.

We climbed into the Jeep, and one of the employees jogged over. "Excuse me, you can't take this vehicle, it's—"

Kirk and I growled at him, and he immediately held his hands up and backed away.

"One employee is already in police custody, don't make it two," Tyler threatened.

It took us forty minutes just to get back to the spot Kirk mentioned, but there was little we could do about that.

Thankfully, we'd packed snacks and water, so we were able to eat and drink while we drove. I knew there was no way Kirk would stop for a snack break.

"Are you sure it was her you smelled, and not one of her friends?" Tyler asked Kirk for the fourth time that day.

"One hundred percent," Kirk said. "She smelled like a strawberry field on a warm summer day. It was so delicious that I froze and couldn't even speak. Then, she shoved her nose into my chest, but got embarrassed about it and ran away."

"What about you?" I asked Tyler.

He ran a hand down his face. "Yeah, I didn't want to admit it earlier, but she smells amazing to me, too."

"So, we're in agreement that the next opportunity we get, we are going to ask her to let us court her?" Kirk asked.

"Yes," I answered immediately.

"If she'll forgive me, yes," Tyler agreed.

"Good," Kirk said. "Because I was going to court her with or without you."

I chuckled and shook my head.

"Wait, there!" Tyler shouted, and pointed to the right.

Kirk hit the brakes and veered to the shoulder so he could reverse back to the small opening in the trees that Tyler had seen.

It wasn't paved, but there were obvious tire tracks going down it.

"It's a start," I agreed, nodding.

Kirk drove down it slowly, head on a swivel as he looked into the woods.

We rolled our windows down to let the air in, just in case we might chance smelling her.

The road was so bumpy that we couldn't drive fast, which turned out to be a saving grace, as a group of men in camouflage ran down the road and we almost ran them over.

I recognized one of them as the guy who'd taken the girls. "That's him," I growled, and unbuckled my seatbelt.

Kirk and Tyler climbed out, and we stood facing the five men before us.

"This is private property," the guy snapped. "And where did you get that vehicle?"

"Where are they?" Kirk asked calmly.

Calm meant he was preparing to attack. Calm meant danger mode was activated.

"We don't have time for you. Get lost," one of the other men snapped and drew a pistol from his hip. He seemed to be the only one with a gun, at least that was visible, but a few did have knives on them. There could be more guns on their ankles, backs, or in holsters on their chests that we just couldn't see.

"Kirk," I warned.

"I see it," he whispered. Standing straighter and exuding as much of his alpha dominance as possible, he demanded, "Where are the women you kidnapped?"

If these men were down this road on foot, did that mean that the girls had escaped and they were searching for them?

Looking around, I tried to see any movement or thing that might be out of the ordinary. Not too far away from the road was a fallen tree, and just beside it lay three yellow helmets like the ones they'd had for the zipline.

I tapped Tyler's shoulder and headed in that direction.

"Hey! Stop! Where are you going?" one of the guys yelled after us, but I didn't bother listening.

"If you don't leave right now, we're going to call the cops!"

"Call the cops," Kirk said. "They're already looking for you. Now, answer my question!"

Stooping down, I picked up a helmet and sniffed it. Not Brooklyn.

Tyler picked up another one and growled softly. "Brooklyn."

I took the helmet and inhaled deeply. Fuck, it was her scent. Closing my eyes, I tried to follow the scent, but it was too faint.

"They were probably running away from those guys, so if

we continue in a mostly straight line, maybe we'll find them," Tyler suggested.

I shook my head. "We have a high chance of getting lost. That's the last thing we need."

Going back to the road to confront the men, we arrived just in time to join the fight.

Kirk knocked the gun out of the guy's hand and punched the guy next to him in the face.

I tackled the one who had driven the girls, punching him in the face until he was unconscious.

Tyler fought another guy, and I barely managed to keep the last guy from punching him in the back of the head.

Panting heavily, I set my hands on my knees as I leaned forward. "Fuck, I'm out of shape."

"Time to get back in the gym," Tyler said, and nodded.

"Let's tie these fuckers up," Kirk said, and put the gun in his waistband, after making sure the safety was on.

"We found a helmet with her scent over there," I informed Kirk.

He growled.

"It's old, though, probably a few hours," Tyler said.

"Why didn't they make it to the highway if it's been that long?" Kirk grumbled. "Once we get her to safety, I'm going to teach her everything I know, so she won't get lost again."

There was a lot I wanted to teach her, but all of it had to do with physical knowledge.

Off in the distance, a woman screamed.

My feet moved before I thought.

Kirk and Tyler were behind me, but I had always been the fastest one.

"How far did that sound?" I asked Kirk, since he was the most knowledgeable.

"Farther than I want," he grumbled.

It didn't matter, I was going to run as far as I needed towards that sound.

"Brooklyn!" Kirk yelled. "Brooklyn, answer us!"

We had to slow our speed to deal with the treacherous jungle fauna.

"Kirk!" Brooklyn yelled.

"Brooklyn!" Kirk yelled back. "Keep talking!"

Another scream, and I knew this one was hers.

"Help!" one of her friends yelled. "Help us!"

The other woman screamed in pain.

What was happening? Why were they screaming? Was a creature attacking them?

"Brooklyn!" I yelled.

Her response was a scream of pain, but her scent hit me in the face like a brick.

Heat. She was in heat.

The pain made sense now. She was in pain because of her heat.

We pushed through a bunch of large plants, and found the three omegas on the ground, writhing in pain, faces red.

"Help," Brooklyn whispered. "It hurts, so much."

"We can't do this in the jungle," Tyler hissed. "We've got to get them to a hospital."

"Why are you all in heat?" Kirk asked, walking around them without getting closer.

"Th-They inject ... injected us with something," one of the other women explained.

"W-Wanted to s-see who was f-f-fertile," the slimmest one explained.

Shit, they really had planned to use them for breeding.

Outrage filled me, but I was more concerned at the moment with the three omegas writhing in pain from their heats being forced upon them.

I didn't even know drugs like that existed.

"I'm going to pick you up, Brooklyn," Kirk told her. "We're going to carry you back to the car and take you to the hospital. We don't know what else they could have given you in that injection. We have to get you checked out."

He was right, there could be something detrimental to them in the injection. Brooklyn whispered something to him too softly for us to hear.

"We're going to pick you up, okay, omegas?" Tyler told the three. "Please, bear with us while we transport you."

Tears streamed down their faces, and it hurt me and infuriated me at the same time.

Kirk picked Brooklyn up and I growled, but shook my head as I reminded myself he was helping her.

Tyler and I picked up the other omegas and we hurried back to the truck.

"Alpha, please help me," the omega I carried begged.

She didn't smell bad, but she didn't smell like Brooklyn. "I'm sorry, we're going to take you to the hospital so they can help you."

After burying her face against my chest, she sobbed softly.

"I'm sorry," Kirk whispered to Brooklyn.

"N-Not your f-fault," she stuttered.

"I should have demanded to ride with you," he said.

She shook her head, but didn't speak again.

Tyler helped get the girls in the Jeep, buckled in the backseat, and said, "I'm going to stay here with these guys. I don't want them escaping while you take them to the hospital."

"No," Kirk barked. "There could be more up at the building."

"Building?" I asked.

He nodded. "Brooklyn said there's a barn up there." He pulled out a pistol. "She shot a couple of them."

"She shot people?" I asked, eyes wide. This omega got more and more interesting as the day progressed.

"Alpha!" one of the omegas yelled. "Please!"

"Tyler and I will check out the building, find a second vehicle, load these bastards up, and take them to the cops," Kirk said. His jaw clenched, and he looked away. "Take care of the omegas."

For him to let Brooklyn out of his sight wasn't something I expected.

"You sure?" I asked.

"I don't want to separate from her, but they need medical help, and I need to punch some more people," he said.

"No killing unless necessary," I reminded him.

Tyler grabbed my arm. "Drive safe, and don't stop no matter how much they plead."

"Maybe it would be better for Tyler to take them. As a beta, it'd be easier to ignore their pleas," I countered, "and he could soothe them a little."

Tyler flinched, but nodded. "He's right. I'll take them." He took the keys from Kirk. "You two stay safe. I'll notify the hospital staff to alert the cops and give them coordinates."

Kirk and I watched him reverse down the road, and I felt like my soul was being torn in two.

"Let's go find people to punch," Kirk growled.

"Are we going to leave these guys here?" I questioned.

They all looked unconscious still, but that could change at any moment.

"They won't be able to get out of those knots," Kirk said. "But, let's take the driver with us as insurance, and as a shield."

I laughed and shook my head. "Sometimes this darker side of you terrifies me."

"Oh, brother, this isn't dark. This is taupe."

I picked up the driver and slung him over my shoulder with a grunt. "Seriously, we've got to start doing our workouts again. I'm far weaker than I'd like."

"You are starting to get a bit of a double chin," Kirk said as he took lead, a pistol in each hand.

"I do *not* have a double chin!"

"It's likely the midlife crisis making you gain weight. It's okay, I'm pretty sure we just found our omega, so you'll want to lose weight to please her better."

"I am not having a midlife crisis!" I growled. "You're the one who was talking about getting a motorcycle just last week."

"You think she'll want to have kids?" he asked as we continued walking up the dirt road. "I know it's harder for women to have children when they're older."

"You're getting ahead of yourself," I reminded him. "We

aren't even one hundred percent certain she's our omega yet, and haven't talked to her about it."

"Oh, I'm certain. She's ours, and I'm not going to let her go."

If he was right, I was going to be ecstatic.

"We'll have to buy gifts to court her," I said to keep the conversation going.

"You think she'd like one of these guys' fingers in a jar?"

"I don't think she'll want a reminder of what happened to them today," I countered.

"Hm," he grumbled. "You're probably right. I want one of their fingers, though."

"Pretty sure the airlines won't allow that through customs," I argued.

"I don't know what she likes," he said softly. "I don't know what type of gift to get her."

"That's why we have to start courting her, to find out what she likes now. The old Brooklyn would have loved books."

"Books? What kind of books?"

"If I remember, she liked fantasy."

"That's good to know. I'll buy her limited editions of all her favorite books. That's bound to win her over."

"Maybe we can start with diamonds until we find out more about what her favorites are," I suggested.

"Diamonds. Big diamonds."

"Every kiss begins with—"

"You are not about to recite a jewelry company's slogan right now, are you?" Kirk asked with a scoff.

The road opened up to a parking area and a large barn.

Two men stood outside the barn next to two other men with bandaged legs, who lay on the ground.

"Time to focus," I said.

"Time to fuck shit up," Kirk countered, and raised the pistols.

CHAPTER 12
Tyler

THE DRIVE to the hospital had been unbearable as the omegas begged me to help them, knot them, bite them, and other things. They even offered to do various acts to try to get me to comply.

I was really glad they were buckled in and I had to drive them.

The hospital staff took the three away and immediately called the cops.

After explaining that the women were in heat due to a drug they were given, the hospital rerouted the omegas to a quarantine area. Apparently, they'd dealt with this before.

"The two alphas from my pack are at the place the girls were taken to," I explained to the cop. He was the one who had taken our statement at the ziplining place. "They wanted to make sure that none of them escaped before you arrived. These are the coordinates."

"Once the omegas are past their heats, we will get their

statements," he informed me. "We don't want to interrupt them or upset them anymore than they already are."

I nodded my understanding and took a seat in the waiting room.

Hospitals creeped me out, and only my worry about Brooklyn kept me inside. They smelled like death and decay, and knowing she was in here stressed me out a lot. Had her heat been a natural one, I would have just taken her back to our hotel, and the guys and I would have helped her through it. Even if she didn't choose us as mates afterwards.

Hospitals meant death to me, and I was close to hyperventilating just imagining her in a hospital room with tubes and IVs strapped to her.

What would I do if I never got to apologize to her? What would become of our pack if we lost her? No, she wasn't our omega yet, but the what-if thoughts would eat us all alive. If she died, I was fairly certain our pack would separate for good.

At thirty-eight years old, I was far too old to deal with the disassociation of a pack again.

When we had separated originally, it was to go after our various dreams. My music career, Buck's football, and Kirk's military. The knowledge that we were going after things others rarely had a chance to attain made the separation easier. Also, knowing we would find each other again at some point.

While out on tour, I hadn't realized how much it would hurt to be separated from my pack. Especially when omegas were throwing themselves at me. I'd thought that was what I wanted, but the truth was, I wanted just one omega. I wanted the one omega that was meant for us.

The tours had been a ton of fun, the women had been fun as well, but the older I got, the more I wanted what I saw in the audience. I wanted *my* omega.

If Brooklyn ended up being our omega, no amount of groveling, apologies, and gifts would make up for the situation I'd put us all in over the years.

Once we had reunited, after my tours ended, Kirk retired from the military, and Buck retired from football, our focus was finding our omega. I couldn't even begin to count the number of dates we had gone on over the last six months. The number of women we had all scouted and tried to get to work.

We had even found one woman we were going to settle for, but she ended up finding her true pack, ones that she was drawn to.

Just like I had always been drawn to Brooklyn.

Just like I was still drawn to her, as much as I didn't want to admit it.

She was gorgeous, even more so now that she was a woman, and I wanted to claim her in every way possible. It had been hard to leave when I'd been listening to them at the bar the previous night.

Hearing her talk about the blind dates, the agencies, and the isolation during her heats was like daggers to my heart.

My fault.

All of this was my fault.

The doctor who had gone with the girls came out a bit later.

I stood and hurried over to him.

He smiled at me. "The three omegas are sleeping peacefully right now. Due to their induced heats, we sedated them. It should pass uneventfully, but we are also running some tests on their blood to make sure there was nothing harmful in the drugs they were given."

"How soon will we be able to talk to them?" I asked.

"A few days, judging by the previous cases we've seen."

Days? I had to wait days to talk to Brooklyn?

"Can I give you my contact information so we can be notified when they're awake?"

"You can give me your contact information and it'll be up to the omega if she wishes to contact you. We aren't allowed to give out patient information or diagnoses, since it's confidential. I only updated you about their condition since you brought them to safety. Leave your number with the nurse over there." He pointed at a nurse at a desk and left.

Getting into a fight with the doctor would do no one any good, so I returned to my seat in the waiting room. I wasn't going to go back to the hotel with Brooklyn here and vulnerable. I would wait to see what room they moved her to, and then wait outside of it. Who knew if there were more people as part of this kidnapping ring that might try to come back for her while she was sedated.

Hours later, Kirk and Buck arrived. I recounted what the doctor said, which made both the alphas growl.

"I'm just going to stay here and guard her room," I informed them.

"We'll go back to the hotel, get provisions, and return," Buck said.

"Why don't we take shifts?" Kirk suggested. "That way at least one of us is with her at all times."

"I like that idea," I agreed with a nod.

"Are you okay?" Buck asked me. "After having to drive them here, I mean."

I blew out a breath and shook my head. "It was hard, man, but I just kept thinking about them being in danger with something else in their systems, and it made it easier to ignore their pleading."

"Sorry you had to endure that," Kirk apologized and set a hand on my shoulder. "You did good, though."

"Did you get to punch more people?" I asked.

He smiled, a purely evil smile. "I may have shot a couple in the legs, too."

Just as the words left his mouth, four men with police escorts were brought in on gurneys.

The men's eyes widened when they saw Kirk, who wiggled his fingers in a ridiculous wave at them.

I laughed softly and shook my head.

"We'll be back," Buck said, patting my shoulder. "Keep her safe."

"Yes, sir."

CHAPTER 13

Brooklyn

I woke up in the hospital, groggy and disoriented.

"Hello, miss," an older male doctor greeted me as he checked my vitals. "How are you feeling? Any pains?"

I tried to speak, but my mouth was incredibly dry, as was my throat.

He picked up a glass of water from my bedside table with a straw in it. "Small sips. You've been asleep for three days."

Three days!

After getting enough liquid to allow me to speak, I asked, "What happened?"

"You were brought in after being injected with a heat-inducing drug. Thankfully, it didn't have any other side effects or issues. We kept you sedated while your heat passed. As long as you're feeling okay now, we can release you to go."

"Wh-What about the others?" I asked, my voice still raspy and sore.

"The other omegas?" he asked.

I nodded.

"They're all the same as you. I'll be going to check on them shortly. Are you friends?"

I nodded again.

"Well, I do know that two alphas and a beta have been taking shifts to keep guard outside your rooms the past few days," he said. "Are they yours or theirs? We were informed you all didn't have packs, but they refused to leave."

Were they talking about Tyler, Buck, and Kirk?

"Ones who saved us?" I asked.

He nodded. "They are the ones who brought you in."

"Friends," I said, and pointed at myself. Why was talking so hard?

"Can I update them on your status? They keep asking, even though we've told them it is confidential."

I nodded, which made him smile. "Excellent. Well, you just keep resting while I check on the others and give us a couple hours of observation to ensure your heat has fully passed, okay?"

"Thank you," I said.

He left, and I closed my eyes. Three days asleep. It was hard to believe I had slept through my entire heat, though I supposed they probably gave me a *lot* of sedatives to accomplish that.

Perhaps that was why I still felt so weak.

Sometime later, a nurse checked my vitals and ensured I wasn't having heat flashes. "Are you up for visitors?" she asked with a smirk.

I nodded slowly, knowing she likely meant the trio.

"Also, you'll have to wait to be discharged until the police come to get your statement, okay?"

I nodded again.

She giggled like a schoolgirl before opening the door and waving them inside. She gave me a wink and closed the door behind them, with her on the outside.

Kirk rushed forward and reached out towards me, but pulled his hand back before he touched me. "How are you feeling?"

"Still a little groggy," I admitted. "And my throat is sore and dry."

"Is your heat over?" Buck asked.

"Yes."

Tyler stood farthest away, eyes downcast and fists clenched.

"Thank you for saving us," I said softly. "If you hadn't come looking for us, I'm not sure what would have happened."

We probably would have been captured by those men again and used as breeders.

"I'm glad we were able to find you," Buck said, and walked closer to me, setting a hand on my leg. "We weren't sure what was happening when we heard you all screaming."

"I thought a leopard got you," Kirk admitted.

"No, not a leopard, thankfully." I smiled up at him and he returned my smile.

"I'm sorry," Tyler said.

My brows furrowed. "What?"

He looked up at me, tears in his eyes. "This is all my fault."

What? How could this be his fault? "What are you talking about?"

"In high school, why were you going to Tony's house?"

That was such a random question, and one I had to think back so long to recall. "Uh, he invited me over to teach me to play drums, but we quickly found out that I have no rhythm."

He looked up at the ceiling. "I was a jealous fool," he said. Dropping his head down so he could look at me, he explained, "Tony was my nemesis, and I thought you were going to his house because you knew that. I was going to introduce you to my pack, to court you, but my jealousy caused me to get my feelings hurt. So, I decided to hurt you back, and that's why I made out with Alysse. I'm so sorry, Brooklyn."

All these years. All these years I had thought he had done it as a cruel rejection, like he ultimately did to Alysse. I'd had no idea.

"I know it may be hard to forgive him, but we're fairly certain you're meant to be with us," Kirk said.

"I'm sorry, I just need a moment to process this," I said, and closed my eyes. All those times I'd argued with them, hated them, had been because of teenage jealousy. All these years alone might have been due to a simple misunderstanding?

"I will spend the rest of my life making up for this in whatever way you want or need—" Tyler said.

"What Tyler is trying to say is that we would be honored if you would let us court you," Buck interrupted.

Court me?

"Y-You three want to court me?" I asked, and opened my eyes to look at each of them.

"We hadn't planned on asking you in the hospital, but

after so long we don't want to waste any more time with you," Buck explained.

"I, um, I don't know," I whispered and clenched the blankets in my fists. "A lot has happened and ... I need some time."

Tyler looked at the floor, dejected.

Kirk scowled, but nodded once.

Buck exhaled and ran a hand through his hair. "Okay. That's fair. You've been through a lot and we can understand wanting some time. We're going to return to the hotel now that you're awake, and we'll wait for you to approach us, okay?"

"Thank you," I said, shocked he agreed to my request.

Buck squeezed my leg once before turning, grabbing Tyler by the shoulder, and leaving the room.

Kirk bent down and kissed the top of my head. "I'm glad you're awake and well. We'll be waiting for you."

Once they left, a wave of sadness smothered me, making me cry uncontrollably.

A nurse came in, and I had to assure her that I was fine, that it wasn't my heat, and quickly wipe my face before talking to the cops.

Two hours later, Stacy, Alexa, and I were finally released from the hospital.

One of the officers drove us to the hotel, where we reluctantly separated, but promised to meet up for dinner.

When I made it back to my room, it was to find dozens of bouquets on each available raised surface, as well as the floor. A few were from hotel staff, my sisters, parents, and Marcus, but the majority were from the trio.

I needed to contact my parents and sisters, but the first necessity was showering and dressing. The hospital sponge bath had not been enough, and my hair was the oiliest it had ever been. It took five applications of shampoo before it was clean enough for me to leave the shower.

As expected, my parents begged me to return home immediately, but I refused since I only had a couple of more days left. Plus, I needed to talk to the trio.

Was I mad at Tyler? Yes. But I also understood it.

Besides, that had happened over twenty years ago.

However, there was anger that I could have been packed up all this time if it hadn't happened.

What would my life have been like if I had packed up with them in high school? Would I have started my business? Would I have ended up pregnant and become like my sisters instead?

The what-ifs were driving me mad.

The most important question was what was I going to do now.

Now, I was going to go meet Stacy and Alexa for dinner. Tomorrow, I would meet with the guys to discuss our next steps.

Tonight, I'd spend it with the women who'd shared a terrifying experience with me.

Stacy and Alexa hugged me as we took our seats at dinner.

"How are you feeling?" I asked them.

"Still a little groggy. I hate being sedated," Stacy grumbled.

Alexa and I nodded our agreement.

"Have you talked to the trio?" Alexa asked. "I wanted to thank them for rescuing us."

"Briefly," I admitted.

"Oh, there is a story there. Spill it, girl!" Stacy ordered with a smile.

I did. I spilled everything. I told them every last bit of information while we drank and ate.

"Oh my gosh, this is like a romance movie!" Alexa squealed.

I scowled. "No, it's not."

"Look, this is your second chance romance, okay? I understand that you're hurt, and you have every right to be, but if you let this chance pass you by, you might truly be single forever," Alexa said, nearly shouting at the end.

"She's right," Stacy agreed. "The chances of you guys showing up at the same resort half way across the world over twenty years later are so low that you cannot discount it. Plus, they rescued you, and us, so you have to give them kudos for that."

"And they guarded our hotel rooms while we were unconscious," Alexa added. "They made sure we didn't get kidnapped by the people."

Sighing and dropping my head forward, I admitted, "I know."

"So, what is the hold up, girl?" Stacy demanded.

"I'm scared." Admitting it out loud was harder than I thought it would be. "What if I get excited, start courting them, and then discover that we *aren't* a match? What if I am really destined to be alone for the rest of my life? What if I fall in love, and they find another omega who they think smells better, and they fall for her immediately and cast me to the side? I can't survive that."

"Bitch!" Alexa yelled, gaining us attention from all of the other restaurant patrons. She pointed at me and narrowed her eyes. "We just survived being kidnapped by psychotic alphas who intended to use us for breeding against our will. We survived the jungle. We survived being stabbed in the arm with a drug that forced our heats to start, and then the doctors put us into a sedated sleep for three days to avoid the repercussions of our heat. And you are telling me, telling us, that you cannot survive being rejected? Girl, how many times have we all been rejected? You will survive if you are rejected by them. But guess what? We are certain that you will not be rejected by them. However, if you are, we will both fly to you, spend the weekend drinking the misery away, and then soothe our sorrows with sweet treats."

My eyes were wide as saucers, mouth dropped open, and a newfound respect forged for her.

"No matter what happens, you won't be alone," Stacy agreed, and reached across the table to grip my hand.

"Just promise us that you won't forget us, and you'll let us come play with your babies if you have any?" Alexa said, smiling wide.

"You'll be the first people I call if I am ever pregnant," I agreed, sniffling as tears threatened to fall.

"Sisters forged in fear and united in midlife crises," Stacy shouted.

"Midlife crises!" Alex and I shouted, and we all clinked our drinks together.

They were right. No matter what happened, I had my

friends, who would stay by my side and help me through anything.

"So, next year we should go on another vacation together," I suggested. "And actually go ziplining this time."

"Yes!" Stacy agreed.

"Sign me up," Alexa said in a deeper than normal voice.

"How about we go to Hawaii this time?" Stacy suggested.

"Agreed," I said, and nodded.

"Yes, please," Alexa agreed.

"Stacy?" a male voice called out.

We all turned and my eyes widened at the handsome man.

He rushed over and knelt in front of her "Oh, thank goodness, you're okay! Your mom told me you were kidnapped, and I feared the worst."

She stared at him, wide eyed and open mouthed before finally looking at us. "Um, guys, this is my boss, Stephan."

"Alexa?" a different male voice asked.

Alexa turned around, as did the rest of us.

"Brandt?" we all asked.

Brandt had been one of the busboys at the restaurant we had met at twenty years ago.

He ran forward and wrapped his arms around her. "Alexa!"

Well, it seemed like my friends weren't as alone as they thought that they were either.

Before long, both were pulled away by the people who had come for them, leaving me alone at the table.

Instead of staying at the table, I carried my drink outside

and walked along the beach. Next year was going to be an interesting reunion.

Ahead on the beach was a lone man, sitting and facing the ocean. It only took me a moment of panic to realize I recognized him. "Tyler?" I asked.

He turned with wide eyes and asked, "Brooklyn?"

Was this fate giving me my chance to speak to him?

I sat down on the sand beside him and joined him in staring out at the sea. We were silent for a long time before I broke the silence. "You destroyed my heart that day. I thought we were just friends, but then our friendship developed more, and I even interacted with Buck and Kirk a bit on a singular basis. The certainty of our courting was something I tried hard to ignore. Then, the joy of it started to fill me up. The night before, I baked you each a dozen cookies, to offer as a gift to accept me for consideration for courting. When I found you and Alysse, I felt like I was literally being stabbed in the heart. I hid away for a week, not even coming out of my room to eat. Then, when I returned to school, I saw my favorite teacher crying because of a prank you caused. I was certain that was my sign that you weren't meant to be my matches. But, try as I might, you kept showing up around me, and so I started treating you as enemies. I wanted to hate you, I really did, but I couldn't. After you left the school, I assumed I wouldn't have to see you again, but you all kept popping up everywhere – on the news, in my newsfeed, on billboards. It took over a decade before I finally started to forget about you. Now, here you all are again and I find out that all of this pain, loneliness, and self-hatred might have been caused because of simple teenage jealousy."

He opened his mouth, but I held up my hand and he closed his mouth again.

"I know you're sorry. I know you would change things if you could, but that's not how time works. Plus, I'm not sure I would want things to change. I love having my own business, and even if we did end up mated, I would never give it up. Do you know, after all these years what my number one concern is about agreeing to you courting me?"

He shook his head.

"It's that I'm going to deepen my feelings for you all and you're going to reject me. I don't know how long it will take me to recover from being rejected by you again. So, I'm going to give you one more night to truly consider if you want to court me or not. Tomorrow morning, I will meet you for breakfast and you can give me your answer then." I stood and brushed off the sand from my butt. "Good night."

Try as I might to sleep, I had lain awake in my hotel room, listening to the sound of waves crashing against the shore and thinking about what all had transpired.

"I hope you're ready," I whispered to myself.

I was about to either make a total fool of myself, or make the best decision of my life, but either way, I figured it was worth the risk.

After all, what did I have to lose?

A tear rolled down my cheek and I quickly brushed it away.

No more crying.

It was time to take action.

Since the day was going to be a momentous one, I showered, fully applied my makeup, and wore the best dress I had brought.

"You are a beautiful, magnificent, and enticing woman," I chanted to myself as I waited for the elevator to open. "They would be lucky to have you."

The elevator doors opened, and before I could scream, the man before me pressed a napkin over my mouth and nose, whatever was on it immediately forcing me asleep.

CHAPTER 14

Tyler

THE RESTAURANT WAS FAIRLY busy for breakfast time, but we didn't care if it was empty or busy. All that mattered was waiting for Brooklyn.

The two omegas who had been with her the day before sat at tables on opposite sides of the restaurant, an alpha we didn't recognize with each of them. They looked happy, which was a good sign.

An hour came and went with still no sign of Brooklyn. Was she still sleeping? Or was she making us wait on purpose, trying to make us feel as anxious as we had likely made her?

"Excuse me," the receptionist from the excursion desk said as she stopped at our table.

Kirk growled, making her flinch back a step.

"What is it?" I asked, giving her a smile, though not as flirtatious as I would have before.

"The woman you asked about? The one who had been kidnapped?"

"Yes, what about her?" I asked, nervousness flooding my system.

She held up Brooklyn's bag. "This was on the ground outside the elevators on the floor of her room and she didn't answer when I knocked on her door. I was going to hold it in case she was just out, but saw you in here and thought it might be better to let you know in case ... something might have happened again."

Kirk sprang up from his seat and ran out of the restaurant.

"Did you see her leave?" I asked.

She shook her head.

"Did you see anyone who looked suspicious?" Buck asked her.

We both stood, and I tossed a few bills on the table for the drinks we'd already consumed.

"Well, there was a man who came in that is usually only here for excursions, but we didn't have any planned. I saw him come in, but didn't see him leave," she admitted. "I thought it was odd, but then assumed maybe he had hit it off with an omega and was here to date her or something."

I grabbed the bag from her and Buck and I ran out of the restaurant.

By the time we reached the lobby, Buck had a security guard pinned against the wall by his throat.

"You will show it to me now, or I will have you added as an accomplice to her kidnapping," he threatened.

The guard nodded, Kirk set him on his feet, and we all followed him to the security office where the camera feeds were.

It took a bit of searching before we found the video of him carrying her out of the elevator on the first floor and out a side door that gave him quick access to the parking lot without going through the lobby.

"It's that asshole who tried to keep us from taking the Jeep," I realized when I saw his face.

"Call the cops, give them the license plate, and tell them what happened," Kirk ordered the guard, who nodded his understanding and started dialing the phone.

"We need a car," I said as we followed Kirk out to the valet area.

"We're going to take one," Kirk said. He reached into the valet box, grabbed a car key that was clearly for a rental vehicle, and stormed out to the parking lot. Thankfully, none of the valets were nearby to witness it or try to stop us.

"We don't know where they've taken her," Buck said. "They aren't going to go back to the same spot, because the police already found them there."

"No, they're going to go to the ziplining place," Kirk said. "I smelled some sour scents coming from there, but had dismissed it as fear from those ziplining. I'm fairly certain it was the omegas they have captive there."

"You're serious?" I asked, despite knowing that Kirk wouldn't lie about something like that.

"I should have trusted my instincts," he growled. "I was too worried about Brooklyn not having shown up yet, and then needing to find her."

None of us spoke as we drove, our anxiousness and worry about her safety too high to allow idle chatter.

Kirk's knuckles were white as he gripped the steering

wheel. Normally, I would have suggested someone else drive, but the alpha was already so on edge that he'd probably take it out on me if I said anything.

So, staying quiet while the former military man formulated a plan was my best option.

I had to grip the handle over the window as he drove faster than the vehicle could handle up the unpaved, bumpy road to the ziplining buildings.

I thought he was going to stop before we got there so we could sneak up on them, but instead, Kirk drove right up to them, almost running over three men.

We climbed out of the vehicle, and Kirk immediately grabbed one of the men he'd almost hit. "Where is she?" he growled.

"I-I don't know what you're talking about, man," he replied with a pale face.

One of the other men stood and reached for a gun at his side, but Buck was already moving towards him, and he grabbed it, pointing it at his head. "Where is the omega they brought here? Where is she?"

"Wh-What omega?" he stuttered with his hands raised.

Buck pulled the hammer back and pressed the gun harder into the man's head. "Tell me, or I blow your brains out," he growled, and the man peed his pants.

"There's a basement in the large building there," he said. "But you won't make it to her. They've all got guns and it's locked."

"Well, thank you for giving me a gun, too," Buck said and slammed the butt of it against his skull. The man slumped back, unconscious, and Buck let him fall.

The third man stayed where he had fallen when he dove out of the way of the vehicle with his hands up.

I walked into the office, grabbed rope, and tied up all three men.

Buck handed Kirk the gun with a nod.

"Do you want me to stay out here and keep watch in case more show up?" I asked Kirk.

"No, we stay together," he said, checked the weapon, and headed into the large building. "Keep watch of our six."

"Yes, sir," I said, for the first time without an ounce of teasing in my tone.

The inside was mostly empty, save for some boxes of gear, as they normally used it for getting people into their gear and providing rules and other information. On the far side was a single door, and even I could smell the sour scent pouring out of it. Mixed among those sour scents was Brooklyn's.

"She's definitely here," Kirk said.

Buck and I nodded.

We stood on either side of the wall next to the door as Kirk pushed it open with his hand. We had to make sure we weren't right in the doorway when we opened it, just in case someone was there with a weapon.

"Clear," Kirk whispered.

He led the way into a small room that had a set of stairs leading down.

"Don't crowd me just in case I need to jump back," Kirk instructed us.

Buck nodded.

Kirk took a breath, checked the gun again, and headed down the stairs.

The stairs were straight for at least two floors, before curving around the rest of the way down.

Kirk held his fist up and Buck and I stopped.

I'd heard it too. Someone speaking.

"What the hell is wrong with you, man? Why would you go back and get her? You know she has people watching her. They're likely going to figure out she's missing and start the search." The person speaking was an unfamiliar voice to me.

"She responded the best to the drug," the one who'd kidnapped Brooklyn said. "Plus, I heard she got into an argument with those alphas and beta, and I saw that beta flirting with the receptionists. I doubt they'll be looking for her."

"Please let me go," Brooklyn pleaded. "I-I'm really not that fertile."

"Well, we're going to find out pretty soon," the kidnapper said. "We don't normally use the drug so close, but time is of the essence, and after we inseminate you, we'll be shipping you off with these others."

There was the sound of metal hitting metal and several unfamiliar women screamed.

Kirk crept forward, gun at the ready.

Buck and I tensed, prepared to run back or jump forward to assist Kirk.

Kirk stepped out and aimed his weapon. "Get that fucking needle away from her right now."

Buck ran out, and I followed right on his heels.

Three metal cells held four women. In the center of the room was a table with Brooklyn strapped to it, and beside her was the kidnapper with a syringe in his hand.

The syringe was empty.

"Fuck," I breathed. "He already injected her."

On the other side of the table were two men, both with a hand on their guns, but not yet drawn.

"I told you," the one who had first spoken growled at the kidnapper.

"Raise your hands above your heads and don't move," Kirk ordered them. "Or, I'll put a bullet between your eyes."

"He'll do it," I cautioned them. "Don't test him."

Buck walked forward, a bit of rope in his hand that he must have taken from the pile I'd brought out earlier.

I headed towards the kidnapper, intent on getting him away from Brooklyn.

Buck took the gun from the farthest guy and tossed it to me.

As it was in the air, sailing towards me, the guy in the middle drew his gun, the barrel swinging not towards Kirk, but towards Brooklyn.

Kirk didn't hesitate as he pulled the trigger and shot the man in the chest.

I caught the gun Buck had thrown and swung it around, slamming the butt into the nose of the kidnapper as he lunged for me.

Blood sprayed, bone crunched, and he screamed.

The last guy stayed perfectly still with his arms still raised. "P-please don't kill me."

"We aren't going to kill you," Buck said, and tied him up.

Aiming the gun in my hand at the head of the guy who had kidnapped Brooklyn, I asked, "What was the drug you gave her just now?"

"Same as last time," he said, his words muffled as he clutched his broken nose. "Heat inducing."

"Shit," Kirk growled. He walked over and undid the restraints on Brooklyn's arms and legs. "You okay?"

She sniffled and shook her head. "Going into heat again isn't good. I don't want to go to the hospital and be sedated. I just started feeling normal again." Her face was streaked with tears and hair stuck to it from sweat.

"I'm sorry," he apologized, and hugged her. "I should have come sooner. Did they hurt you? Any injuries?"

She shook her head again. "Used chloroform in the elevator, and I woke up here." She looked down at her clothes. "No, I'm not injured."

I grabbed one of the leather restraints off the table and used it to bind the hands of the kidnapper. His face was already swelling up from how hard I had hit him with the gun.

Part of me wished I'd hit him a little harder, and more than once.

Buck searched the men to find the key to unlock the cages and free the other omegas. They flinched away from him as they exited, all running for the stairs.

"Can I carry you?" Kirk asked Brooklyn.

She nodded. "Please."

Instead of carrying her bridal style, he had her face him, wrapped her legs around his waist, and supported her butt with one arm. This allowed him to keep hold of the gun in the other hand.

"Let's go," Buck said.

I nodded and took point, heading up the stairs with the gun in front of me, just in case.

"We should take you to the hospital," Kirk whispered to Brooklyn.

"No, please don't make me go back. They'll sedate me again."

"What do you want us to do? Your heat is going to hit soon. We can help you through it if you want, but I don't want to pressure you. There are clinics nearby as well."

I clenched my jaw to keep from saying anything. This was her choice, so we had to let her make it, even if the thought of her going to a clinic to ride out her heat made me sick to my stomach.

"Are you sure?" she asked. "I haven't gone through a heat with others before."

"We can help you through it, no strings attached," I told her while I kept walking up the stairs. Looking back at her would likely cause me to trip on the steps, and the sooner we got her out of this place, the better. "Setting up ground rules will help us ensure we don't cross any boundaries you're not comfortable with."

She was silent, which worried me, but we reached the top of the stairs, and when I looked back, I saw she was thinking. I also saw that she had her nose pressed right against the side of Kirk's neck.

Lucky bastard.

After dealing with the cops, omitting that Brooklyn had been given the drug again, we returned to the hotel and to our room.

Brooklyn took a long, hot shower and put on a pair of my shorts and one of Buck's shirts.

Kirk made her some hot tea and sat beside her on the couch.

She leaned against his side while she drank the tea. "Thank you for saving me, again."

"You don't need to thank us." Buck set a tray of cheeses and meats on the coffee table. "We're glad you're safe."

"How did you find me so fast?" she asked, looking at each of us.

Was she scared we were part of it?

"One of the hotel staff found your purse outside the elevator and brought it to us. Kirk had one of the security guards check the footage, and we recognized the guy who kidnapped you as one of the employees at the ziplining place," I explained.

"We figured they weren't going back to the original place, and I realized the sour scents at the ziplining location we'd gone to likely were from the other omegas." Kirk smiled down at her. "I'm really glad I was right about that."

She smiled back at him. "Me, too."

"I'm going to grab provisions," I said, and stood. "Is there anything you want in particular? Or something you usually crave?"

"Mint chocolate chip ice cream and lemonade," she requested, her eyes lighting up as she said it. "Oh, and cheese, salami, and crackers." Right after saying it, she leaned forward and grabbed a piece of cheese off the plate. "Swiss and Colby Jack are my favorites."

"Okay, I'll be back," I said, grabbing my wallet.

The hotel was abuzz with the information and I knew they would have to increase their security in the future, now that someone had been kidnapped from their location.

Brooklyn's two omega friends ran up to me with tear-filled eyes.

"Is she okay?" the smaller one asked.

I nodded. "She's fine. Resting now."

"Poor Brooklyn," the other sniffled. "I can't imagine what I'd be going through if I was taken a second time. Will you tell her to find us or call us when she's available?"

"I certainly will." I gave her a smile and continued on my way to the little shop that had snacks for sale. Unfortunately, they didn't have anything she wanted, so I called a taxi to take me to the grocery store. I didn't care if I had to go to another state, I would get her whatever she wanted.

CHAPTER 15

Brooklyn

I STAYED IN THE GUYS' hotel room for a full twenty-four hours, but my heat never came, not even a hot flash.

They'd done a great job of keeping me sidetracked by asking about my life, my business, my family, and telling me about themselves.

Being with them felt easy and natural, but after we were sure my heat wasn't hitting, I excused myself to decompress in my hotel room alone for a while.

We had all carefully avoided the courting subject, as well as the misunderstanding that had occurred in high school.

As I sat on my hotel room balcony, staring out at the ocean, I started thinking about it again.

There had to be a discussion on what they expected of me if we did court or end up mating. We lived in neighboring states, so someone would have to move. If I moved, that would mean moving my business headquarters as well. I knew most of my employees would not be up for a relocation, especially not the mated omegas I had on staff.

My parents and sisters had freaked out even more when I told them about the second kidnapping, but I figured it was better they learn from me than the news. Dad had demanded I come stay with them, but when I informed them that I was meeting with a potential pack, they had all shut up.

Because that was their ultimate goal, after all.

Exhaling harshly to try to rid my body of the annoyance I didn't want to harbor felt good.

Out on the beach, I caught sight of three familiar male figures carrying boogie boards out with them.

They were incredibly nice to look at, and also just incredibly nice. Tyler had even gone into town to get the food I'd requested yesterday. Something I felt bad about, because I hadn't ended up going into heat.

The guys removed their shirts, set them down on lounge chairs, and continued out into the water, smiles on their faces as they talked.

What would life be like with them? Kirk was retired, and focusing on hobbies like woodworking. Tyler was living on the royalties from his music and tours, but also creating music in his private studio at their mansion, and posting it on music sites. Buck was doing his motivational speaking, and coaching, and had a video gaming hobby.

How could I incorporate myself into their lives?

How would they incorporate into mine? At the moment, I spent a lot of time in the office or working on new plans and designs. Would they be interested in helping me with my business?

Too many questions without answers only made me irritated.

The urge to do something, anything, hit me, and I quickly messaged Alexa and Stacy in the group chat we had created.

Me: Let's do something wild.
Stacy: Such as?
Alexa: How wild?
Me: Let's go get tattoos!
Stacy: That's wild to u?
Alexa: Matching?
Me: Yes! To commemorate our renewed friendship
Stacy: This is clearly the midlife crisis talking for U
Me: o.o Rude AF
Alexa: Well, my midlife crisis is answering her call. Let's go!
Stacy: I found a shop yesterday with good reviews
Me: U beezy! U were planning to get 1 already
Stacy: I figured 1 of U would want some ink
Me: Pick me up from my room. K?
Stacy: K
Alexa: kk

I'd promised the guys I wouldn't leave my room alone, and that I'd message them when I was going somewhere. So, I sent a quick message telling them I was going to a tattoo place with the girls and got my shoes on.

Alexa knocked using a secret knock she developed, which was just three quick knocks done twice in a row.

I double-checked through the peephole to confirm it was her before I opened the door.

"Tattoo time!" she shouted and looped her arm through mine as she pulled me out into the hallway with Stacy at her side.

"How far is the shop?" I asked.

"It's a five-minute drive and the taxi is already waiting for us," Stacy informed me.

"Awesome!" I shouted.

"Do you know what you want to get?" Alexa asked.

"I was thinking we could get something small on our wrists," I said, since I had not had time to really think of something.

"What about simple piña colada glasses?" Stacy suggested. "You know, an outline of the glass with a straw, pineapple piece, and the little umbrella?"

Alexa and I both dropped our mouths open simultaneously.

"Yes!" I shouted as we stepped into the elevator.

"You're a genius," Alexa praised and pushed the button for the lobby.

"They shouldn't be too expensive, either, if we just do a small outline in black," Stacy said, her cheeks bright red from our praise.

"Oh my gosh. I'm so excited. These are going to be the best midlife crisis tattoos ever." Alexa squealed as we made our way through the lobby and out to the waiting taxi.

Five minutes later, we sat inside the tattoo shop, waiting for the artist to prepare a station to do our tattoos.

Our artist was an attractive alpha with bright blue eyes, a

bald head, and tattoos covering almost every inch of visible skin. "You know, usually it's packs getting matching tattoos. It's refreshing to do them on friends."

"Second chance girlmance and joint midlife crises necessitated matching tattoos," Alexa said, and smiled at him.

Oh, she was totally into the tattoo artist!

"So, you guys don't have packs? I can't imagine your alphas letting you out alone like this after the kidnappings that just happened. Poor girls."

"Actually, that was us," Alexa said and shrugged her shoulders. "This is part of our old maid, sisterhood, post-trauma, bonding experience."

He stared at her like she'd sprouted a second head, his hands paused mid wipe of the table.

"It's okay. We were lucky to have escaped quickly," I added with a shaky laugh.

"Whoa, I'm glad you girls are okay. Um, that's ... wow." He quickly finished setting up and applied the outline to all of us on our wrists. "Let me know now if you want the placement changed or anything. Once we start, it'll be too late."

We stood next to each other, arms down and pressed together with our matching outlines on. Yeah, this was perfect.

"I'm good," I said.

"Me, too," Stacy said.

Alexa nodded with a huge smile. "Yep! Let's do it!"

An hour and a half later, we had new tattoos covered by plastic with instructions on proper care.

"How much will it be, Tom?" Alexa asked as she pulled out her wallet from her crossbody bag with a cute kitten on it.

She had asked him a ton of questions while he'd done our tattoos, not even giving Stacy or me a chance to talk to him. It was adorable to witness her enthusiasm.

"Free," he said.

"What?" all three of us asked simultaneously.

He smiled. "Consider them gifts, and my hope that you won't view all alphas negatively just because of a few bad seeds."

"Are you sure?" I asked. "We appreciate the gesture, but—"

"I'll only accept it if you go out to dinner with me tonight to further prove that statement," Alexa said.

Stacy and I stared at the usually meek woman suddenly being bold.

He smiled, grabbed the paper that he'd originally drawn the design on, and wrote his number down. "I look forward to dinner."

The three of us headed outside to the waiting taxi and climbed inside. We were silent all the way back to the hotel and up to my room. As soon as the door shut, we spun to face Alexa.

She squealed, grabbed our hands, and we all jumped up and down with her.

"My heart was about to beat out of my chest!" she squeaked. "But, oh, he smelled so *good!*"

"I'm so proud of you!" Stacy praised and hugged her.

"What about Brandt?" I asked.

"Oh, he's a lone alpha," she explained. "So, um, he agreed to let me keep my options open, and even build my own pack."

Whoa! I hadn't heard of that before.

"That's great," Stacy said.

"How are things going with your guys?" Alexa asked. "They saved you yet again."

"Yeah, there are a lot of things I have to work out still," I said, and sighed. "Speaking of that, I'll let them know I'm back and probably go to dinner with them."

"I've got a dinner date with Stephan," Stacy said. "So, I will say goodbye for now. I love my new tattoo, and love that I'll have a piece of you girls with me everywhere I go."

We had a long group hug before they left.

I messaged about dinner in the group chat with the guys and a few minutes later had Buck at my door.

"Hello, beautiful," he greeted, and kissed my cheek.

His scent drifted into my nostrils and I inhaled deeply. "Hello, handsome."

"How was your outing?" he asked, and stepped back so I could exit my room.

I held up my arm for him to see.

"A piña colada?" he asked.

My smile grew impossibly wide. "Yep. We all got matching ones, and we even got them for free."

"Whoa, nice," he said, pushing the button for the elevator.

"Alexa even got a date with the artist! I think this trip has helped her come out of her shell a little more."

"That must have been scary to do," he said. "She likely had the courage because you were there with her."

"Maybe," I said, not having thought of it that way.

"Kirk and Tyler are getting a table for us," he said, and

stepped closer to me, brushing some of my hair behind my ear. "I'm tempted to steal you away for some alone time, though."

Heat rushed to my core and face simultaneously. "Your pack wouldn't be happy with you."

He dipped his head down and drew in a deep breath with his nose right next to my ear. "They'd forgive me. God, you smell delicious."

"So do you," I admitted, gripping his shirt, and pulling myself closer to him, inhaling deeply from his neck. "I didn't think anyone could smell this good."

"If we don't separate, I might make good on that threat," he whispered in a deeper voice.

Just as I was about to give in to my desire to lick him, the elevator doors opened.

I stepped back, my face completely on fire, and hurried out of the elevator, trying my best to ignore the smirks of the people we had to walk by who had seen us.

Buck caught up to me easily with his long strides and led the way to the outdoor restaurant.

Tyler and Kirk stood when we got to the table. Both kissed my cheeks before Tyler pulled out my chair for me.

After showing them the tattoo and ordering drinks, I decided to draw on the courage Alexa had expressed.

I set my menu down and looked at each of the handsome men in front of me. "I have questions before I agree to courting."

All of their eyes widened.

"Go on," Kirk urged.

"Would you be willing to move to my state? Or would

you expect me to move to yours?" I asked. "My business isn't capable of being relocated at the moment."

"I would need to stay through the current football season," Buck said. "I wouldn't want to abandon the kids midseason."

"Tyler and I can do our stuff anywhere, really," Kirk said. "So, we have no problem moving."

"I would want to ensure we had a proper place to stay before we moved," Tyler said. "I need to get a recording studio set up right away."

Wow, they really were willing to move for me?

"You didn't expect those responses, did you?" Buck asked with a smirk.

"Honestly, no," I admitted and chuckled.

"Okay, what other questions do you have?" Kirk asked.

"Will you be willing to let me continue with my business, even if I end up pregnant?"

"Would you be willing to let me work with you or at least work in the same building as you?" Kirk asked, a huge frown on his face.

My eyes widened. Work with me? I had wondered if they would be interested in helping with my business. I wouldn't want to give him a stupid job or anything, so maybe giving him an office next to mine he could use for whatever he wanted was a compromise I could accomplish. I did have several open offices at the moment.

"An open office might be available," I said hesitantly. "I'm not sure what open positions you would be interested in, though, so I might be willing to let you use one of the offices for yourself."

"I'm only thinking of your safety," he explained quickly. "My dads couldn't stand to let my mom out of their sight when she was pregnant and I have no doubt I'll react the same. It's already hard to be away from you." He said the last sentence quietly with his eyes down, so I didn't think he meant for me to hear them, but I had.

"We can discuss it more if it happens," I said.

The waiter brought out our drinks and took our order, forcing us to pause our conversation.

"Any other questions?" Tyler asked.

Dropping my eyes to my glass so I could avoid their eyes, I asked, "What if I end up unable to have a baby?"

"We can discuss any options you are okay with. Surrogacy, adoption, anything," Kirk answered immediately.

My head snapped up. "Serious?"

Tyler smiled softly and nodded. "Yes."

I looked at Buck who nodded. "We can answer for each other. We've talked about all of this a lot over the last year alone."

"Wow, okay." I didn't think they'd answer all of my questions in a way that I agreed with.

"Can I ask you a question?" Kirk asked.

"Yes." I sat up straighter, wondering what he could want to ask me.

"Are you willing to learn about our hobbies? Maybe participate in them?"

"Oh, yeah! I love learning new hobbies. Though, I've got no rhythm and am a terrible singer so Tyler might find it harder to share his hobby with me."

All three laughed.

"Are you willing to split holidays between families or rotate?" Buck asked. "We usually make sure to split them up and swap between during the years and we definitely want to include your family in that."

"Oh, for sure!" I agreed. "Plus, it'll be nice to go to a few different families instead of just mine like I have been."

"What's your favorite holiday?" Tyler asked.

"Thanksgiving!" I shouted a little too loudly for being in a restaurant.

An omega at a nearby table laughed at me while Tyler, Buck, and Kirk smiled.

"That's good to know," Kirk said.

"Any other questions for me?" I asked.

"Favorite gemstone?" Tyler asked.

"Gemstone?" I asked back and tapped a finger against my chin as I thought. "Sapphire."

"Favorite dessert?" Buck asked.

"Favorite dinner?" Kirk asked.

"Favorite candy?" Tyler asked.

I laughed and held my hands up. "Whoa, slow down. One at a time and let me answer first."

"Sorry," they said simultaneously.

All four of us laughed.

We continued to laugh and learn more about each other for the rest of the dinner, through dessert, drinks, and dancing at the beach bar. It wasn't actually a dance bar, but after eight o'clock the drinks had been flowing, and the patrons started dancing just outside the bar. We weren't to be excluded and although I wasn't the best dancer, I was too inebriated to care what I looked like.

They took turns dancing with me, their hands roaming along my body and in my hair.

"Will you come back to our room?" Tyler requested, his hands on my hips as we danced to a slow song.

"Your room?" I asked and lay my head on his chest. "Sir, are you flirting with me?"

"I thought that's what I'd been doing all night," he said. "Perhaps I'm off my game. I thought I'd been doing so well."

My head fell back as I laughed and I looked up into his eyes. "Do you really think this is fate?"

He slid a hand along my cheek, beneath my ear, and around the back of my head. "I don't care what it is as long as it's not a dream I'll wake up from." Bending forward, he pressed his lips against mine.

I fisted my hands in his shirt and kissed him back. His scent surrounded me and, in that moment, only he and I existed.

He licked the seam of my lips and I opened my mouth willingly, our tongues meeting in a slow, explorative dance.

It wasn't until my back hit the inside of the elevator wall that I realized I'd climbed up his body, wrapped my legs around his waist, and he'd carried me inside while never breaking our kiss.

A second set of hands stroked my back and I reached out a hand, trying to touch them.

This had not been the plan for today, but I wasn't going to stop now. I wanted them, needed to taste them, and I was going to enjoy myself doing it. Well...I hoped I would.

Once in the hotel suite, Tyler set me down on one of the

beds which smelled like Kirk so I assumed it was his room, and stepped back.

Tyler, Kirk, and Buck stood before me with hungry expressions on their faces.

"We want to hear you say you're consenting before we move forward any further. If you think you're too drunk for this, we'll stop right now," Kirk said.

I stood up, pulled my shirt off over my head, and shimmied out of my pants. Standing before them in only a bra, I drank up the hunger and pheromones flooding the room. "I want you, all three of you. But I have ground rules. No claiming tonight, okay?"

"No biting," Kirk agreed, and the other two nodded.

"No knotting either," I added. Although I wanted a baby, I wanted an official pack first. The last thing I needed was to get pregnant and then have them leave me.

"Okay," Buck agreed and Kirk nodded.

As a beta, Tyler didn't have a knot, so he didn't need to respond.

"Anything else?" Tyler asked and pulled his shirt off with one hand in a singular swift motion that had me salivating.

"Condoms," I said quickly. I wasn't a virgin, and I highly doubted these studs were either.

Tyler disappeared into one of the other rooms in the suite and returned with three condoms.

Kirk stepped forward, rested a hand against my cheek, bent down, and tenderly kissed me. The tenderness quickly morphed into fire as he claimed my mouth and wrapped his large arms around me, surrounding me in his scent. All I could smell was Kirk and I wanted to drown in it.

I pawed at his shirt, desperate to touch his skin, to rub my face against him.

Buck pressed his warm, bare chest against my upper back and I arched into him. I could feel his erection against my lower back. Reaching a hand back, I stroked him through his jeans.

"Too many clothes," I growled.

"Oh, I like that growl," Buck said. He pressed his mouth against my shoulder and growled down at me. "Do it again."

My slick had already soaked my thong and was starting to drip down my inner thighs.

Buck, now shirtless, grabbed my hands and placed them on his chest. He was incredibly muscular, built like a power-lifter, and I let my hands drift down to his stomach. "He gave you an order, omega. Growl again."

Unable to ignore a direct order, I obeyed, and growled. My hands dipped lower, stroking him through his pants.

He was large, so large I was worried about him fitting.

"Don't worry, sweetheart, I'll warm you up plenty before I try to fit this in you," he said.

"Are you a mind reader?" I asked and frowned up at him.

He smiled. "No, but most women have that reaction to me."

Why did it upset me to have confirmation that he had slept with other women? Was it because...

No, I wasn't going to focus on that. Not now.

I unbuttoned his pants with a snarl, jerked them down, bent over, and took his head into my mouth.

"Fuck," he growled and slid his fingers into my hair.

"Reposition," Tyler barked, though, since he wasn't an alpha, it didn't carry the compulsion of an order.

Still, everyone complied.

Kirk pulled out of my mouth with a pop and moved all the way up the bed until he sat against the headboard. He crooked a finger at me. "Come to me, little omega, and put that pretty mouth on my cock again."

I had started walking on my hands and knees across the bed, but paused. "Please?" I asked, waiting for him to add the phrase.

He smiled and his cock jumped. "Please put that pretty mouth on my cock again."

Precum dripped out of his head and I licked my lips, eager to lick it up and swallow him down again.

Just as I did so, Tyler slid on his back up the bed and suctioned his mouth to my clit.

I moaned around Kirk's cock, making him groan and grip the headboard with both hands, his hips bucking up slightly before he caught himself.

Buck climbed onto the bed, his hand slapped against my butt, though not too hard. "I've wanted to do this since we were sixteen years old." He slid his hand down, his fingers dipped into my folds, and two slipped into my wet core.

I jumped in surprise.

Tyler grabbed my thighs, keeping me still while he swirled his tongue along my clit, tingling and throbbing already.

Carefully, I took more of Kirk in, down my throat until my lips hit his knot, never taking my eyes from his.

"Fuck, Brooklyn. You do that too much and I'm liable to come like a virgin," he said.

Buck pumped his fingers in and out of me while fondling one of my breasts. "No coming until she does," he ordered.

Sitting up enough to look behind me, and take a breath since Kirk was so large, I let myself get a good view.

Tyler licked and sucked on me while he stroked himself.

Buck fingered me and squeezed my breast, occasionally squeezing my nipple, and gripped his rock-hard cock in his hand.

"Can I take a picture?" I asked, although not intentionally out loud.

"No, but we can do this again if you enjoy it," Kirk said.

I turned back and dove down, swallowing him all the way to his knot.

"F-fuck," he hissed and threw his head back so hard it smacked into the headboard.

"Yes," Buck said. "Just like that, little omega. Please the alpha while we please you."

Tyler's licking finally hit that crescendo and I jerked against his mouth. Buck and Tyler held me in place, refusing to let me up as they milked my orgasm out. My slick poured out, down Buck's fingers and my legs onto Tyler's chest.

"Oh, hell yes," Tyler breathed as he licked my legs. "Again."

Buck straddled Tyler's stomach and lined up with my entrance. "My turn." He entered me slowly, all the way until his knot pressed tightly against me.

I moaned and arched my back. A warmth I'd never experienced before built and pulled within me.

Kirk gripped my hair at the back of my head and started fucking my mouth.

Tyler stroked himself faster as he licked me again, my sensitive nub already ready for round two.

Buck gripped my hips and set a hard and steady pace, his knot pounding against my entrance with every thrust.

"Come for us," Kirk ordered. "Come on Buck's cock and scream around my cock."

Immediately, my orgasm hit, making me see stars as I screamed around him and my muscles tightened around Buck.

He groaned and quickened his pace. "I can't last long," he admitted. "She's too wet and tight."

I wanted to tell him to knot me. I wanted to tell Kirk to bite me. To claim me.

I was glad my mouth was occupied.

CHAPTER 16
Tyler

Brooklyn orgasmed again, her slick pouring into my mouth and I drank it all down, licking up any that I missed.

Buck grunted and shuddered above me. "Oh, shit."

Never had he finished so quickly. We had shared quite a few women over the years, and this was definitely an abnormality.

"Switch," Kirk ordered.

Brooklyn gasped for breath as we all separated from her. Heat radiated off of her, her pheromones pumping out like crazy. Her scent called to me in a way that I had never experienced with a woman before. As a beta, I shouldn't have been so affected, but here I was, drawn to her like a moth to the flame. Wanting, no needing to help her get whatever pleasure she wanted.

"More," she begged. "Please."

Was ... was she in heat? But there had been no indication earlier.

No, she must just be enjoying herself.

I could understand. It had been several months since I'd had sex, and this was definitely an enjoyable experience.

Kirk took Buck's spot, while I took Kirk's spot, more than ready to have the beautiful woman suck my cock. It was something I'd thought about constantly in high school. Now, it was finally going to happen.

As soon as I sat down in front of Brooklyn, she licked her lips at the sight of my hard cock. It was so hard, it actually hurt.

"What are you waiting for?" I asked with a teasing smile. "He's standing at attention for you, waiting for those pretty pink lips."

"You want me?" she asked, giving me a teasing smile of her own and licking her lips suggestively.

"Oh, you have no idea," I told her. "I masturbated at least four times a day in high school, every single time thinking about you."

A flicker of pain flashed across her face before she smiled and backed her butt up, spearing herself onto Kirk's cock. "Then you can wait a few minutes longer."

Her head flew back in ecstasy as the large alpha worked himself in and out of her, deeper and deeper each time until she could fit him all the way up to his knot.

"That's right, sweetheart. Take all of me just like that." Kirk gripped her ass and growled. "So fucking hot."

Her face was red as she met each of his thrusts with her own.

"Buck," I whispered, getting his attention, since he was still staring at her after throwing away his condom.

"Hm?" he asked.

"Her face..."

"Yeah, it's fucking glorious watching her."

"No," I said and sighed. "She looks like she's in heat."

Buck's eyes widened, and he looked back at her. "Oh, shit."

"Maybe it's just a hot flash," I suggested.

We all knew she'd been given those drugs. Maybe it had taken longer to activate this time.

"What's wrong?" she asked, panting. "Do you ... not ..."

"I'm just waiting for you to stop teasing me and put that mouth to work for something else," I said.

She dropped her upper body down, swallowing me all the way to the base.

I gasped and gurgled on my own spit as her hot mouth and throat closed around me.

My hips had a mind of their own, pumping up into her mouth as my eyes rolled up into the back of my head.

Kirk set a bruising pace behind her, their skin slapping together loudly in the room.

Buck whispered into Kirk's ear and his eyes widened as he set a hand on the middle of her back.

Brooklyn took that as instruction and lowered her upper body down more, angling her ass up.

Kirk growled in satisfaction and forgot all about Buck's words as he increased his speed.

Brooklyn's tongue swirled around my cock each time she pulled back, and bliss unlike anything I'd experienced filled me. I wasn't going to last. I wasn't going to be able to hold back enough to fuck her this time.

And oh, there would be another time. Now that I had a taste of her, I wasn't going to let her go.

None of us would. She was ours.

She just didn't know it yet.

CHAPTER 17

Brooklyn

Like a lucid dream, I spent two days sleeping with the trio, never leaving their room and barely letting them leave.

Apparently, the drug I'd been given had taken longer than usual to induce my heat, but when it hit, it hit like a son of a bitch.

The four of us lay on the bed, panting, covered in sweat and slick, and weak.

"I-I'm sorry," I whispered. My heart pounded quickly and my breaths came quickly, even though we hadn't moved in an hour.

"It's not your fault," Kirk said. "Don't apologize."

"I'm going to go get food for us," Tyler said and stumbled to the bathroom.

Buck smoothed sweat-sticky hair away from my face. "Are you okay?"

I nodded. "More than okay. That was ... amazing."

Kirk chuckled. "Careful, you might give us even bigger egos than we already have."

"Thank you," I said. "And especially for ignoring my pleas." Halfway through our time together, I'd started begging them to knot me and claim me.

They had somehow resisted.

I knew at least twice Tyler had to intervene, to stop Kirk and Buck from claiming me.

"We should shower," I suggested.

Kirk stood, gathered me in his arms, and carried me to the large bathroom, Buck right behind us.

"Should we wait for Tyler?" I asked, feeling bad for leaving the beta out.

"No, he can shower later," Kirk said. "You need to get clean and dressed so you don't get sick."

I wasn't certain how I'd get sick, but I didn't argue.

Buck turned on the shower, waiting until it was hot before he nodded and stepped in.

Kirk set me on my feet, keeping a hand on my lower back.

I didn't think it was necessary, but realized that my legs were very jelly-like from all of our vigorous fun.

Buck grabbed a bar of soap and started cleaning me.

Kirk washed my hair, scrubbing my scalp with his fingernails.

This.

This was what I had craved all these years.

A pack to take care of me. A pack to provide me support.

And holy fuck was this amazing.

I wanted this forever.

But ...

Was this really something I could have with this trio?

Sure, the sex had been mind-fucking-blowing, but that wasn't all that was necessary.

"You're scowling awfully hard for someone getting cleaned by two hot guys," Buck commented.

I scoffed. "Conceited much?"

"Duh," Kirk replied, gripped my hair, and pulled my head back so he could look into my eyes. "Talk to us, beautiful."

"I'm trying to just live in the moment, to enjoy this, but ..."

"But that's hard with all the questions and uncertainties between us," Buck guessed.

I nodded.

Kirk kissed my cheek. "It may be hard, but let's focus on the here and now for a bit longer, okay?"

I nodded my agreement, took the bar of soap from Buck, and started scrubbing him down.

Once we were all clean, dry, and dressed, we sat on the couch to watch some television.

"Oh, where's my phone?" I asked, realizing that due to my heat I had ignored it for two full days.

"Here," Buck said, reached to the side table, and handed it to me.

As expected, there were dozens of missed calls and messages.

"Oh, shit," I gasped. "I missed my flight back home and overstayed. I was supposed to check out yesterday."

No wonder my family and Marcus had called so many times.

After quickly letting them know I was safe and fine, that my heat had hit unexpectedly so I'd been indisposed, that quieted them.

"Are you hungry?" Kirk asked, brushing hair away from my face as I looked up at him.

I nodded. "Yes, but I don't really want to leave right now."

The hotel door opened and Tyler smiled at me. "Lucky for you, I have returned from the hunt with provisions."

"Hunt?" I asked, and laughed.

He started talking like a neanderthal. "Ho, ho, yes, I great hunter. I get food. Food for pretty lady."

As he set plastic bags of food on the table, I patted his head. "Such a good little hunter."

He snapped his teeth at me playfully, which made me laugh.

Once I was fed, I leaned into Kirk's side.

He raised his arm, letting me rest my head on his chest, and started purring.

I had heard about alphas purring, had seen my dads do it with my mom, but for the first time I was able to experience it, and within minutes was fast asleep against him.

Sneaking away from the guys was the only way to extricate myself from them. The hotel staff was understanding of my predicament and had allowed me to keep my room for a few days longer than I had originally scheduled. Probably partially due to the fact that I had been kidnapped on their property, and they didn't want to get sued.

Tomorrow morning, I would be leaving, taking a plane back home.

"There you are," Buck said as he joined me at the bar for a drink and kissed me on the cheek.

"Hello," I greeted. "Sorry, but you were all so exhausted that I felt bad and didn't want to wake you."

"Was the hotel manager nice to you?"

I nodded. "He extended my stay, so I am checking out tomorrow."

He scowled. "You're leaving tomorrow?"

"Yes, my flight leaves early in the morning," I answered.

He glared down at the bar top without speaking.

"Brooklyn! Oh my god! Brooklyn!"

I turned around, eyes wide as I stared at Marcus running towards me, dropping his suitcase in the middle of the restaurant to spread his arms for a hug.

I got off the stool and ran to him, meeting him halfway.

He threw his arms around me and hugged me tight. "You're okay, you're really okay."

I hugged him and patted his back. "Hello, Marcus."

He pushed back, holding me out at arm's length. "Don't you hello Marcus me, you bitch!"

Buck growled, stood up from the stool he had been sitting on, and marched towards us.

"It's okay," I said and set a hand on Buck's forearm. "He's a friend."

Marcus looked between us a moment, eyes wide, leaned

forward giving me a big sniff, and then gave me a devilish smile. "Oh, you little minx! Why didn't you tell me you had packed up?"

Buck's eyes widened.

"Oh, I'm not packed up," I replied immediately.

Buck growled softly, but looked down at his feet.

"Marcus, this is Buck, a friend from high school and one of the men who saved me from the kidnappers. Buck, this is my best friend, Marcus. He works with me at my business."

Marcus scoffed.

"Okay, Marcus runs most of my business for me," I amended.

Marcus shook hands with him. "Nice to meet you."

"You as well," Buck said with a nod of his head.

We headed over to the bar and Marcus sat on my left, while Buck returned to his seat on my right.

"How are you feeling? Is your heat officially over? Please tell me you're pregnant." Marcus spouted off the sentences so quick I couldn't reply.

Buck had started to drink his martini, but the last statement had him choking on it and sputtering.

I smiled and shook my head. "Not pregnant, sorry to burst your bubble."

Marcus sighed. "Your mom is going to be so disappointed and I owe your sister twenty dollars."

Why was I not surprised?

"Did they send you here to check on me?" I asked.

He nodded. "Plus ..." He grabbed my hands in his. "... I was worried about you."

"Your job is safe," I assured him with a pat on his cheek.

He exhaled harshly. "Thank goodness! Bartender, a tequila shot, please. No, three shots, please."

I laughed and shook my head at him. "Did your boss approve your vacation? I'm fairly certain she wouldn't."

He growled at me. "Listen here, you tyrant, I was working like a dog for a week, dealing with frantic calls from your family about you going missing, the media wanting information on you, and those tabloid leeches showing up at our building! If anyone deserves a vacation now, it's me. You owe me."

"How about I buy you that new VR headset you've been raving about?" I suggested. "Will that calm your ire?"

He stuck his hand out. "Shake on it?"

I shook his hand.

"Yes!" he shouted. He leaned around me and scowled at Buck. "So, what's your problem? How come you rejected this perfect specimen back in high school? Are you stupid or slow or just an idiot?"

"Marcus!" I gasped and smacked his arm.

"No, he is asking fair questions," Buck said and leaned on the bar top to look at Marcus. "Honestly, we just weren't in the right place mentally to accept her. She was feisty and I wanted a meek omega. Now, I couldn't imagine wanting anyone less than her."

"Wh-What? Don't say things like that or I'll get the wrong impression," I said and fanned my suddenly hot face.

Buck smiled. "Oh, baby, I'm pretty sure the past two days have shown you exactly how we feel about you, and have given exactly the kind of impression we wanted."

"That was just your alpha instincts responding to my

omega heat," I countered and waved at the bartender. "Another drink, please!"

"Is she always this dense?" Buck asked Marcus.

"I blame you three," Marcus growled. "You fucked her up good from high school."

Buck raised his hands. "Not my fault. That's all on Tyler."

If a blush could kill, I would be melted right now. "Shut up!" I said and squirmed in my seat.

"So, are you one of the reasons she said she can't relocate her business?" Buck asked Marcus.

Marcus looked at me with narrowed eyes before looking at Buck. "Yes, and I will fight you if you try to force us to move."

Buck held up his arms in surrender. "I didn't say we were. I was just wondering who it was she was thinking about when she mentioned not being able to relocate. I was worried it was a man, but it seems you aren't interested in her in that way."

"No, she's my long-lost sister, definitely not someone I'm interested in. Wait, are you going to move to her? For the love of all that is holy please buy a new place. Hers is small and full of books with little room for anything else. She needs a library and a separate office so she can function. I can recommend a really good realtor if you're interested."

"Marcus!" I hissed.

"I'd love your realtor," Buck said, pulling out his cell phone at the same time Marcus did.

"There you two are," Tyler said as he walked up behind

me. He wrapped his arms around my waist and hugged me. "Why are you stressed out right now?"

Marcus turned, looked Tyler up and down, and said, "Oh, you're *him.*"

"What does that mean?" Tyler asked, stepping back from me a bit.

"You're the reason—"

I slapped a hand over Marcus's mouth. "If you speak one more word right now, I will cut your salary in half!"

Marcus's eyes widened, and he nodded once against my hand.

"What is he talking about? Who is this guy?" Tyler demanded.

"Are you guys hungry?" Kirk asked as he joined us.

Marcus's eyes widened when he saw him.

"Not a single word," I hissed.

"What's going on?" Kirk asked.

"Maybe we should leave," I suggested to Marcus and started to stand.

Buck put his arm around my shoulders and kept me on my stool. "No, we are going to use this last night with you to get to know Marcus."

"Last night?" Kirk and Tyler asked simultaneously.

"She's flying back home tomorrow," Buck informed them. "This is Marcus, her best friend and right-hand man at her business."

"No sexual intention!" Marcus shouted a bit too loudly, gaining attention from nearby patrons.

Kirk held out his giant hand for Marcus to shake. "Nice to meet you."

"Let's get some food," Tyler suggested. "I know Brooklyn has to be hungry right now."

No. I was definitely mortified.

Marcus slipped his arm through mine and pulled me out of the bar. "You are as red as a tomato, and I'm going to commit this to memory. It will be the one thing that gets me through any rough patch in my life. I'm going to laugh about this, even while I cry over not having an omega."

"I'm going to murder you in your sleep," I threatened.

He patted my arm. "You wish, princess."

The guys paid our bill and followed us out.

"Please lead the way. I just arrived, so I don't know where anything is," Marcus instructed. He leaned his head against my shoulder. "I'm just so glad my fearless leader is safe and sound."

I bared my teeth at him and hissed.

"Oh, very snakelike. We could totally use that for social media posts. Can you do that again when we're back at the office?"

"Ten percent docked," I threatened.

Marcus mimed zipping his lips closed.

"How long have you worked for Brooklyn?" Kirk asked as we headed towards the last restaurant I hadn't tried yet.

"Oh, I think I'm at my ten-year mark now, right, boss?" Marcus asked and batted his long eyelashes at me.

I narrowed my eyes at him. "No, it's nine years."

"Oh, so I'm close to the ten-year raise mark!" he said happily and squeezed my arm in a hug. "So exciting!"

"Yes, and based on your performance today, you'll get a zero point zero zero zero one percent raise," I hissed.

Buck laughed. "Don't be like that, Brooklyn. We just want to learn more about you, and he is the first person we've encountered who can tell us more. It's not his fault we're asking him questions."

"Oh, it is one thousand percent his fault," I countered.

"How many men has she brought to the building?" Kirk asked out of the blue.

Marcus frowned. "None, but I do know she was signed up for five agencies and at least three apps for finding a pack. None of those worked out, and the alphas she did meet were complete losers. Like, couldn't even hold a job for more than a few months kinds of losers."

"That's terrible," Buck said and looked at me. "No wonder you're still single."

"Oh, how's your midlife crisis going?" Marcus asked as we waited for a table.

I showed him my new tattoo. "My friends and I got matching midlife crises tattoos since we survived getting kidnapped together."

He examined it and nodded. "Totally fitting. I remember you stumbling into work with one of those in your hand one summer day."

My mouth dropped. "That was because I was on vacation and *you* called me in!"

He shrugged. "Sure it was. So, how was your heat? Was it enjoyable?" Marcus asked and waggled his eyebrows.

"Shut up," I grumbled and pinched his side.

"Ouch," he hissed and laughed.

They took us to a table and Marcus took the seat on my left before anyone else could.

Kirk scowled and sat across the table from us, while Buck sat on my right. Tyler sat beside Kirk, across from me.

"So, if you aren't packed up, are you at least courting?" Marcus asked.

"Um..." Were we? I had discussed it, but had we confirmed it?

"Yes," Kirk answered. "She agreed to court us, but we're still working out the details."

Details like how could they court me from a different state definitely needed working out.

"Oh, she's awful about details," Marcus said and waved his hand dismissively. "Tell me what you need set up and I'll handle it."

"How is your omega search going?" I asked Marcus.

He smiled. "I actually think I may have found my pack."

My jaw dropped. "What! Why didn't you say anything?"

"Well, I was a little busy dealing with your news here," he said, and rolled his eyes. "The alpha and beta have been friends since high school and we all get along really well. We're going to start our omega search as a pack soon."

"That's so exciting! Congratulations!" I hugged him tightly and ignored the growl from Kirk.

"What time is your flight tomorrow?" Kirk asked.

"Early, seven a.m.," I answered.

"Be warned your family is aching to take you to the cabin and lock you inside," Marcus said. "Your dad almost flew out here himself, but when I offered to do it, he relented and stayed home."

I cringed. "I do not want to go to the cabin. I'll go straight to my house instead and video call them."

"Where do you three live?" Marcus asked.

"Texas," Buck answered.

Marcus made a face. "Oh." He looked at me. "Thank you for not relocating us to Texas."

I rolled my eyes. "You're welcome."

"Real estate is way cheaper," Tyler pointed out. "We've got a mansion there, but moving to California for the same price would be what, a mobile home?"

Marcus and I laughed.

"There are some areas that are cheaper than others."

"You get what you pay for," Marcus said with a shrug. He looked at Buck. "I'll give you some city suggestions, and I can even map out some areas to look in."

"Hey, we don't know that we're going to pack up yet," I reminded him. "You're putting the cart before the horse."

Marcus put his arm around my shoulders and squeezed. "Inhale positivity and exhale self-doubt. You're beautiful. You're a catch. Any pack would be lucky to have you."

I took in a deep breath and exhaled. He'd started doing these motivational mantras to help me a few years ago. They did help, surprisingly, and that's why I started incorporating them into my products.

"If they decide not to pack up with you, I will take you to Tokyo on that vacation you've always wanted to mend your broken heart. I don't think they're that stupid, though. This is their second chance just as much as it's yours."

"Right, but that didn't mean we were actually meant to be together."

"Well, that's why you're courting," he reminded me. "So you can find out." He looked at Kirk. "When do you plan on coming out? I'll adjust her calendar to make sure she doesn't have anything planned, then."

"We haven't discussed it yet," I said quickly. "Stop pestering them."

Buck took out his phone and searched through something. "How does her calendar look in two weeks?"

"Two weeks?" Kirk asked, and growled.

"I have the camp next week, which I can't miss, remember?" Buck said.

Marcus took out his phone, opened our team calendar, and nodded. "That can work. Do you want a hotel suggestion or…" He looked at me. "You should just let them stay at your place."

"My place is too small. There's nowhere for them to sleep," I reminded him. I looked at the guys. "I only have a twin bed and no spares and only one couch that wouldn't fit Kirk laying down."

"I bet your dad would love for them to stay at the cabin," Marcus said, and smiled evilly.

"You put that suggestion to them and I will kill you," I snapped.

The waiter came to take our order, pausing our conversation, but Marcus immediately resumed it by telling them which airport to fly into and where to stay so they could be close to me and the office.

Buck set a hand on my bouncing leg and rubbed his thumb across my thigh. "This would have been a lot easier if we'd found you in our state instead of being on vacation."

"Nothing is ever easy," I said, and then bit my lip. "Sorry."

Marcus flicked my forehead. "Bad."

Kirk growled at Marcus.

I rubbed my forehead and stuck my tongue out at him.

"Oh, I brought you a present," Marcus said. He scrolled through his email on his phone, found the one he wanted, and held the phone out to me.

After reading through it, my eyes nearly popped out of my head. "Y-You got us a slot on TV? On the morning show?"

"Yep," he said, making the p pop as he said it. "I think that deserves a bonus."

I threw my arms around him and squealed. "I give in. You can use the fancy title you've always wanted."

He pushed me back into my seat and asked, "For real? I can be Chief of Marketing and Digital Design?"

"We can draft up new org charts when we get home," I promised.

"Yes!" he cheered and pumped a fist in the air.

Our food came and Marcus told me about the newest drama in his world. His family was huge, so there was always drama happening and he loved dishing it out to me.

Buck, Kirk, and Tyler just watched us silently.

"I'm going to go lay out in the sun while I can," Marcus said after we finished our meal. "Don't keep her up too late, boys." He thrust the handle of his luggage into my hand and left.

"Sorry about him," I said as I turned to face the trio. "He's ... energetic, but means well."

"You guys seem close," Kirk said.

I nodded. "He's my best friend."

"You and he ever ..." Kirk let the question hang.

I pretended to throw up. "Definitely not. Like he said, we're basically siblings."

"What's your plan for the rest of the night?" Tyler asked.

"I need to pack," I said. "But other than that, I don't have any plans."

"Can we help you?" Buck asked.

"Help me pack?" I'd never had anyone offer to help me pack before. "It won't take me that long. I didn't bring much with me."

"Why don't you come to our room after you finish packing then and we can hang out?" Tyler suggested.

"Okay," I agreed.

Kirk leaned down and rubbed his cheek along mine, pressing a kiss against it before he turned and walked away.

"He okay?" I asked. The big guy seemed out of sorts.

"Yeah, he just doesn't like the idea of being separated from you for so long and us being so far away," Tyler explained.

Well, there was little I could do about that. I had to go back home and work.

"It's only two weeks," I said softly because even though it should have been fine, I was feeling anxious about being away from them as well.

We took the elevator together, but separated when I got to my floor.

Once in my hotel room alone, I flopped onto my bed and sighed. Was my nose right? Were these guys my mates? Was there really a point to courting?

Thinking about the next two weeks had me breaking out in a sweat. Two weeks away from them without their scent, touch, or sight. Well, I could likely get them on video calls to see them. It wouldn't be the same, though.

CHAPTER 18

Kirk

Two weeks away from Brooklyn would be torture.

"Are you sure I can't just go ahead of you all and—"

"Bro," Tyler said and shook his head. "You're obsessed, and it's not a good look."

"This is how they said we would feel when we found our omega," I reminded him.

It had taken a lot of self-control not to pull Brooklyn's chair around to our side of the table after having to watch Marcus touching her. I understood they were friends, but he was a heterosexual male, an alpha, and therefore a potential threat.

"We have a lot of things we need to take care of," Buck reminded me. "First and foremost is buying courting gifts."

"Courting is pointless. We know it's her we want," I growled and slouched on the couch.

"Yes, but we have to convince her that *we* are who *she* wants," Tyler said.

"You should buy her two courting gifts. One to apologize

for being an ass and the second as the actual gift," Buck said as he continued browsing on a jeweler's website.

"He's not wrong," I agreed.

"I'm thinking Marcus is our ticket to perfect courting gifts," Tyler said.

I growled.

Buck shook his head. "I don't understand how you're so much more possessive than me when we're both alphas."

"Because I know what it's like to lose people and I don't want to allow any opportunity to emerge for us to lose her," I said.

The guys knew bits and pieces of my military history, but I hadn't told them all of it. I'd lost a lot of good people and close friends in my twenty years there. Some haunted me to this day.

"We also need to give her some space to figure things out on her end," Tyler said. "She would have to move to a bigger house for us all to live together if we do end up mated."

Oh, we were going to end up mated. I was going to ensure it.

"What if she gets into an accident and we aren't there?" I asked.

"You can't lock her in a tower," Buck reminded me. "She's not the type of woman to allow that."

Instead of groaning about it more, I took out my laptop and started searching for gifts for her. My first option was a bookstore that specialized in limited edition signed books.

One thing I intended to do when we got our new house was build her a library. Bitches loved libraries. Okay, she wasn't a bitch, and I was glad I knew that now, but it was a funny saying I'd picked up from the internet. Honestly, I wished I had known how amazing she was when we were younger. I might have just stolen her out from under my friends' noses.

"You've got that evil look on your face. What are you planning?" Buck asked.

"I'm not plotting anything," I replied immediately.

"You were," Tyler accused.

"I was just thinking about how I would have stolen her from you when we were younger had I known her better then," I admitted.

Buck jumped across the table and knocked me to the floor. He tried to put me in a headlock, but no matter how strong the former football player was, he wasn't trained or skilled enough to best me in wrestling.

"Winner gets first cuddles," I growled as I locked my ankles around his legs and successfully put him in a chokehold.

"No ... fair," he panted and elbowed me in the side.

"I may be pudgy now, but I've still got enough muscle under there to keep that from actually hurting. You're getting weak. You need to get back to working out."

"Your mom needs to work out," he huffed and pried at my fingers to try to loosen my grip.

"My mom is a wonderful lady. You take that back," I said and tightened the hold, cutting off his airway.

Tyler jumped into the fray, trying to take advantage of my occupied limbs. "You huge brutes are such trouble," he grunted.

"Hello?" Brooklyn called as she peeked her head inside

the door; we'd left it slightly open so she didn't have to knock. Her eyes widened when she saw us.

"Hey," I wheezed out as Tyler wrapped an arm around my throat.

"Um, is everything okay?" Her face was red as she watched us, and the scent of her arousal slid into my nostrils.

"Just ... playing," I assured her, and choked Buck hard enough he tapped my forearm in submission. With him out of the way, I reached back, grabbed Tyler, jerked him forward, and rested my fist against his forehead. He held up his hands in surrender.

Leaping up to my feet, I brushed my clothes down and smiled at her. "All done packing?"

She nodded and looked at her feet. "Yeah."

"Want to watch some TV with us?" I offered, standing before her with her scent floating into the room, I wanted to rub all over her, to cover myself in her scent and cover her in my scent.

"Okay," she agreed, and raised her head. Her eyes widened, and she reached a shaky hand up to touch my lip. "You're bleeding."

I hadn't felt it and it didn't hurt currently, but I still went to the bathroom to look. My lip was slightly split. Must have happened with Tyler jumping in.

"It's okay. It's just a minor cut," I said.

I turned around, and she was there, her arms reaching out to wrap around me. She hesitated since I'd turned around, but I didn't hesitate.

I wrapped my arms around her, pulled her into a tight hug, and inhaled from the top of her head. "Hey."

She rubbed her face against my chest. "Hey."

"Two weeks is going to be hard," I whispered.

She nodded. "I know. But ... it shouldn't be, should it? We've been apart for twenty years and just reunited. I shouldn't feel so anxious to be away from you for just fourteen days."

"Technically, it's thirteen," I admitted. "I feel the same, though. The thought of not smelling you or touching you for that long is almost painful. My logical brain is telling me that's an insane way to feel, and maybe I shouldn't admit that to you, but I don't want to hide anything from you, and that is the way I feel."

Her anxiety was building, and I felt her tremble slightly.

Without conscious thought, I started purring.

"Can we sit down?" she asked in a soft voice.

I picked her up, continued to purr, and carried her out to the couch.

Buck and Tyler's brows rose as they saw us.

I gave a single shake of my head to let them know not to ask and sat down with her in my lap.

She pressed her face against my throat. "Um, can I, uh, ask for something weird?"

"Weird?" I asked, mind racing with all kinds of options.

"Can you take your shirt off?" Her face was pressed against my neck so I couldn't see it, but I felt the warmth against my throat and guessed she was blushing.

I leaned forward, making her sit up, and removed my shirt. She rubbed on me like a cat, which in turn made me purr louder.

After she had her fill of rubbing, she lay her head on my

chest, listening to my purr, and relaxed. The scent of her anxiety disappeared and I smiled over at Buck, who flipped me off.

"What will you do for the next two weeks?" she asked.

"Me?"

She nodded against my chest.

"I'll likely be stressing out, pacing around the mansion, finding the perfect courting gift for you, and worrying about your safety." I told her I wanted to be honest with her and I meant it.

"We'll likely be doing something similar while also keeping him from flying out to see you ahead of our planned visit," Tyler said.

She turned and looked at Tyler. "Are you sure about this?"

He frowned. "About what?"

"Me," she whispered. "You all seemed indifferent to me in high school and—"

"Oh, we weren't indifferent to you," I countered, interrupting her. "I wanted you, but shoved it down since you were being such a thorn in our side. We were all too immature to handle you back then, but oh, I definitely wanted to."

"I know I can't change what I did, but I will spend the rest of our lives trying to make up for it," Tyler said, reaching over and setting his hand on her cheek. "I want you. I've always wanted you. You smell like heaven."

"You'll have to move," she whispered. "You'll have to make sacrifices to be with me."

"Every relationship is about compromise," I said.

"Moving back to California will be nice. I've been looking for a change of pace and place."

"I work a lot," she whispered. "Even when I'm home, I'm working on new ideas and plans."

"And I'll ensure you're eating and hydrated when you do," I said quickly.

"We'll help you with work if we can, too," Tyler said. "We don't know much about your business or how we *can* help, but we will do our best."

"What about—"

I gripped her chin between my finger and thumb and tilted her face up to look at mine. "We exist to make your life easier, better, the best it could be. We have gone through the last twenty years establishing our income and selves. We are perfectly set up to move to you, assist you with your business, and be at your side. The only thing that remains to be confirmed is whether *you* want us to make it official or not." I growled when she opened her mouth to speak and she closed it. "I'm not asking you to give us the answer right now. I'm just letting you know how we feel."

She was silent for a bit, simply resting her head against my chest and listening to me purr.

I had never purred for anyone before. It felt ... good.

"I'm scared," she whispered. "I don't want to have my heart broken."

She stopped talking, but we could all hear the *again* she didn't say out loud.

Tyler left the living room and retreated to his bedroom.

"We're scared, too," Buck admitted to her. "That's why we have the courting period, to get to know you better."

She exhaled softly and nuzzled my chest.

I purred louder.

Several minutes later, I realized that her breathing indicated she was asleep.

Tyler returned, sat beside me, and set a hand on her thigh. "I fucked up."

"Yes," I agreed.

"She's mostly forgiven you," Buck said.

"You just have to heal the wound you've caused," I said softly.

Talking made me stop purring, and she stirred at the disruption.

I resumed purring, and she sighed softly as she settled again.

How could someone captivate me so much and yet I barely knew them? These alpha/omega bonds made absolutely zero sense. We viewed them almost like magic, not questioning them despite the weirdness of just *knowing* who you would be mated to by scent.

There was no doubt that Brooklyn smelled divine to me, unlike any woman before her.

Utterly strange to think about.

"Buck," I whispered, "take over so I can go pee."

Buck took his shirt off, tossing it across the room, and took Brooklyn. His purr wasn't as deep as mine, but Brooklyn shoved her nose into the side of his throat, listened to his purr, and settled quickly.

"Ours," I whispered as I stood.

Buck wrapped his arms around her back and nodded.

Tyler ignored us, continuing his search of houses in some of the areas Marcus had mentioned to him.

Our beta was trying, and I had to hand it to him, he was handling things better than I expected.

Together, we would convince her that we were meant to be and get her to accept our bonds.

No matter what it took.

CHAPTER 19

Brooklyn

"Sorry, guys, but I've got to take her from you," Marcus said, waking me up from my amazing sleep on a super warm and delicious smelling pillow.

Buck and Kirk growled, startling me fully awake.

"What is it?" I asked, sitting up and looking around.

A few seconds of processing later allowed me to determine I had been asleep on Tyler on the couch in their hotel room and Marcus stood at the door with his arms raised in a placating gesture.

"What time is it?" I asked, and rubbed a hand down my face.

"Five a.m. and we have to check out and get to the airport," Marcus said.

"Oh!" I gasped and stood quickly. "I'm sorry, Marcus."

He smiled. "It's fine. I already have your bag and took the change of clothes you left out." He held them out to me. "Go get changed. I'll wait right here."

I took the clothes and hurried to the closest bathroom.

Kirk followed me inside. "Are you sure you have to go back to your place? You could come to ours, fly to our home, and stay with us for a few weeks."

That idea did sound fun, but ...

"I'm sorry," I said as I changed, looking at him in the mirror over the sink. "I've got to get back to my business. We've got several big things happening that I cannot miss. I wish the timing was different. I really do."

He spun me around and pinned my lower body against the sink with his. "I don't want to be apart from you."

I set my hand on his massive chest and smiled up at him. "I know. It's definitely going to be rough, but distance makes the heart grow fonder, right?"

He growled and kissed me deeply.

When he pulled back, he rested his forehead against mine. "Promise you'll keep us updated."

"I'll let you know when I get to the airport, when I fly out, when I land, and when I get home. You do the same?"

He nodded and exhaled harshly. When he stepped back, I nearly changed my mind seeing his erection in his pants.

He growled and stalked out of the bathroom.

I quickly brushed my hair and teeth and ran out to Marcus, who took my clothes and put them inside my suitcase while I hugged each of the guys.

"Don't forget about me while we're apart," I teased, blew them a kiss, and all but ran out of the hotel room and towards the elevator.

Marcus jogged after me, laughing. "You're acting like your tail is on fire."

"If I don't leave now, I might very well stay with them," I

whispered, and rubbed my hands together as we waited for the elevator.

"I wish we didn't have this launch, or I'd tell you to just go, but I really, *really* don't want to do this launch by myself," he said.

"It's fine. This is my business and I've waited thirty-eight years to find them, so I can wait two weeks longer." I sounded much surer than I felt.

We made it to the airport and through security just in time to board our flight.

I sent a chat in the group chat and let them know I had boarded safely. I also sent one to Alexa and Stacy, who didn't respond.

Likely because they were still asleep.

"Next time, don't let me take such an early flight," I grumbled to Marcus as I relaxed and closed my eyes.

"Yes, boss," he said with a laugh.

"Can you please silence your phone?" Marcus growled as we sat in a conference room to discuss the final details of my launch.

"They're just excited for me," I said with a smile as I pulled my phone from my pocket.

"Annoying is more like it. How are they dealing with the separation?"

It had only been three days since I returned from vacation, but it felt like an eternity. The guys kept suggesting moving up the date they arrived, but I couldn't let Buck miss out on the stuff he already had planned.

"About as well as I am," I admitted. "It's almost ... painful, but seeing them and hearing their voices helps."

Speaking of seeing, I scooted my chair closer to Marcus's and held my phone up to take a selfie of us both. "Smile!"

Marcus made a goofy face instead of smiling, which made me laugh and was a great picture. I sent it and Tyler immediately sent back a smiley face with hearts for eyes.

Kirk sent back a crying face.

Buck didn't respond since he was working.

"Okay, put the phone away. Time to work," Marcus ordered me. "Don't make me lock the phone up."

"Oh, I dare you to tell Kirk to his face that you're going to take my phone away so he can't talk to me."

Marcus scoffed. "I do not have a death wish, thank you very much."

I laughed and put my phone back in my pocket on silent. "Okay, it is on silent and in my pocket. Now, we can focus on the project at hand."

Only, I couldn't focus very well and Marcus ended the meeting after he'd flicked me in the forehead thrice.

"Boss, why don't you just fly out to them? You're not any good to us like this. You can attend meetings by video and take care of things virtually while I take care of things here. We already accomplished all the things I was worried about before. You're just causing me stress at this point." He set his hand on my shoulder and smiled at me. "You should be with them right now, being courted, and getting to know them better."

Kirk had suggested multiple times that I could come to them.

"I don't know," I whispered, and looked at the carpeted floor.

"We both know that there's not much else for you to do since you pre-recorded the television spot and organized the team. You have a good team and you should trust them. Now, why don't you go pack up your work laptop while I find the first available flight to Texas?"

He was right. I should be with them, I should go to them, and get to know them all better. Scent and magical bonds were important, but I wanted to know them, to fall in love with them.

I kissed Marcus's cheek and power walked out of the conference room and to my office. It took me a stupidly long time to find my laptop bag and the charging cable, but once I did, I packed it all up and grabbed my notebook, shoving it inside the bag as well.

"You've got a flight in two hours. It's the last one for today," Marcus said as he entered my office.

"I haven't packed!" I shouted, panic flooding my system.

"Girl, you don't need to pack. Just fly there and buy some clothes once you get there."

He was right that I could do that.

"Okay, but I need to let them know—"

I pulled my phone out, but Marcus set his hand on top of it. "Wouldn't it be more fun to surprise them? I'll schedule a private car to pick you up from the airport and take you to their house."

My brows furrowed. "You have their address?"

He nodded. "We were discussing the realty situation and Buck gave it to me."

After giving him a big hug, I hurried out of the office, to the parking garage across the street, and into my car.

This was it. I was really doing it. I was going to fly and surprise them.

I wanted to surprise them, to update them, but instead kept my phone in my pocket. No, I didn't want to ruin the surprise and since I didn't want to lie to them; I needed to ignore them for now.

Traffic ate up so much of my time that I had to sprint to the gate to board my flight. The stewardess smiled at me as she scanned my boarding pass. "Going to see prospects?"

I nodded and straightened. "Yes, we just started courting."

Her eyes widened. "Goodness, girl! Why aren't you with them? Get on the plane, go!" She handed me my ticket and then talked into a walkie talkie, but I couldn't hear what she said as I hurried down the ramp to the plane.

The stewardess at the plane guided me to an open seat in the front row. "Here you go, ma'am."

"Thank you," I said, shocked there was a seat available in the front.

She winked. "We've all been there. Being away from prospects is hard."

I nodded. "It's only been a few days and I can't get rid of this constant pressure."

She nodded and tapped the center of her chest where I felt it. "I was away for three days before I caved and rushed to them."

"Today is three days," I admitted, and my cheeks heated in a blush.

She laughed and patted my shoulder. "You'll be okay, hun. I'll get you a water with ice as soon as we're airborne."

Buckled into my seat with my laptop bag stowed overhead, I closed my eyes and exhaled slowly.

Would they be happy to see me? Would they be mad I surprised them?

Kirk might be mad I got onto a plane without telling him.

Would he forgive me when he got to hug me?

As I rode the escalator down to the transportation area, a familiar giant male stood in the check in line.

"Kirk?" I called out.

He turned with wide eyes as he spotted me. "Brooklyn?" He shoved between two alphas, ignoring their growls as he rushed over to me. He sniffed me a bit and then enveloped me in a hug. "Brooklyn! What are you doing here? Why haven't you been answering your phone?"

"I came to surprise you," I said, my voice muffled by his chest and shirt.

He leaned back, picked me up under the butt, and raised me up until I could wrap my legs around his waist. "I'm definitely surprised. I was on my way to surprise *you*, actually." He kissed me deeply, our tongues tangling together, and I moaned into his mouth.

"Sir, if you're unmated, I'm going to need to ask you to leave. The omega's scent might stir other unmated alphas," a security guard said.

Kirk growled as he broke our kiss. "Let them try to touch her and I'll break their hands."

I set my hand on his cheek and smiled. "Kirk, can you take me to your home?"

He nodded and carried me out of the airport. I knew there was no point in asking him to set me down, so I pressed my nose into his throat and inhaled as deeply as I could.

"You sure I'm not dreaming?" Kirk asked as he headed towards the parking garage.

I licked his throat, and he stopped walking.

"You do that again and I might get us arrested for indecent exposure," he growled.

"Sorry, I'll behave, alpha," I said.

He purred. "Call me that again."

"Call you what, alpha?" I asked in a high-pitched voice.

He moaned. "Dammit, woman. You're going to get me arrested."

I laughed and leaned back so I could look at him. "I know it's the hormones or pheromones or whatever makes us stupid little omegas tick, but I am so happy to see and smell you."

He kissed my lips gently, barely a butterfly of a kiss. "You have no idea how happy I am to see you, too."

"Can we keep my being here a secret until we get to the house, to surprise Buck and Tyler?" I asked.

He nodded. "Whatever you want, sweetheart. I'll go tear the heart out of that guy if you want me to."

The guy he pointed to paled and walked faster into the airport.

I smacked his chest. "Behave, sir."

He set me down beside a beautiful bright blue truck and opened the passenger door. I climbed in and was shocked into stillness as he reached around me to buckle my belt and shut the door.

After walking around, buckling himself in, and starting the truck, he looked over at me and smiled. "I still can't believe you're here."

I reached my hand out and let him link our fingers together. "Me neither. A few hours ago, I was in a conference room in my office with Marcus, taking selfies to tease you."

He growled and drove us out of the garage. "I did not like that picture."

"Why not?"

"Because he was with you while we couldn't be."

"Will the others be happy I'm here?" I asked softly. Yes, I'd been super excited to come here, but now that I was here, I was worried they wouldn't actually be happy to see me.

"Of course they will be," he said immediately. "And if they aren't, I'll beat some sense into them and take you around to see all the sights."

My stomach growled, and I set a hand on it. "I am hungry. They only had small snacks on the flight."

"I'll make you whatever you want when we get home," he promised, and squeezed my hand.

"You cook?" I really knew so little about them.

He nodded. "It was one of the first things I learned to do. My mom and grandmother loved cooking for the family and they spread that joy to me. I usually make the holiday meals wherever we go. My favorite is cooking turkey for Thanksgiving and goose for Christmas."

"You're making me really hungry," I said with a chuckle.

"Well, we better get you to the house as soon as I can then, huh?"

We lapsed into silence, and I relaxed in my seat. Silence with Kirk was comfortable. I enjoyed just being next to him.

He drove well and I lost track of time as we went through the unfamiliar city.

My eyes nearly popped out of my head when we pulled up to iron gates and down a tree-lined drive that led to a ginormous mansion.

They hadn't been kidding when they said they lived in a mansion.

"This is huge," I gasped.

"That's what she said," he quipped before hopping out of the truck and running around to open my door.

There was no way they could get the same type of place in California. Not for at least triple the price.

"I can't believe you would even consider leaving this," I whispered.

He linked his hand with mine and led the way through the garage and into the house. "The only thing we need is you. A house isn't what's important, it's what is inside the house that matters."

We walked into the house, through an amazing kitchen,

and to a living room where Tyler was being photographed shirtless with three gorgeous women in bikinis.

My heart plummeted at the sight, and I stopped in my tracks.

What was this? Why was he with these women taking pictures?

One of the women set her hand on his chest and smiled longingly up at him, batting her eyelashes.

Kirk growled, making everyone spin around to look at us.

Tyler saw me, and his eyes widened. "Brooklyn."

I backed up a step, pulling my hand free from Kirk's. This had been a mistake. This was all a mistake.

"What is this?" Kirk demanded.

Tyler walked across the room, his eyes wide and almost like he was in a daze. "Brooklyn, is that really you?"

I ran back through the kitchen, out the garage door, and stole the truck Kirk had just driven, glad he'd left the keys inside.

CHAPTER 20

Tyler

"WHAT THE FUCK IS THIS?" Kirk demanded and grabbed my upper arms.

"It's a photo op for my upcoming release," I choked out. "Was—"

"Yes, that's Brooklyn," Kirk said and turned around. "Wait, where did she go? Brooklyn!"

"She ran out," I said, and tried to get his hands off me. "Let me go. We have to go after her! It's a misunderstanding."

Kirk punched me in the face, knocking me to my hands and knees, and stars danced across my vision. "If you just fucked this up for us, *again*, I'm going to fucking kill you."

No. No, this was a misunderstanding. I wasn't doing anything wrong, I was just ...

"Are you okay?" one of the women asked as she knelt by me, setting her hand on my arm.

I smacked her hand away and ran out into the garage, grabbing the keys to my sports car as I went. Once my car started and my phone connected, I called Brooklyn, but she didn't answer. I called again and again as I raced down the road, looking for any sign of her.

She didn't know this town, so where could she have gone? Had she driven back to the airport?

No. I didn't think she would.

I called her again, but this time it went straight to voice-mail. She'd turned her phone off.

Because of my jealousy, I hadn't asked for Marcus's phone number, so I couldn't even call him.

Calling Buck was out of the question. He was working and didn't even know she was here, let alone what had just transpired, and the last thing I wanted to do was pull him out of work just to come kick my ass.

Kirk called my phone, and I answered. "Did you find her? Did she call you?"

"I used the tracking app for my truck. It took me a minute because I forgot my fucking password. Where are you at?"

"Driving by the Whataburger."

"You're closer to her than I am. The truck is parked at Seventh and Dalton. Fix this, or I'm severing our pack." He growled the threat and hung up.

Swallowing hard, I tightened my now sweaty grip on the steering wheel.

If our pack broke apart again, I wasn't sure what I would do. I wasn't sure I would be able to function. They were my best friends, my lifelines. If I lost them, it would be like losing my right arm. When I'd been on tour, away from them and thought we would never find each other again, I'd done a lot of things to cope. Drinking, drugs, and trying to fill that hole with women, but none of it helped or worked.

I thought we'd never find each other again, but we had, against all odds.

I would not lose them now. I wouldn't lose them because I wasn't going to let this chance with Brooklyn slip by again. This was my second chance with her, and I was not going to let it slip through my fingers.

She was here. She had flown to visit us, which meant she wanted to be with us. It meant that she craved us just like we craved her.

I pulled into the parking lot, found Kirk's truck, and climbed out of my car.

Brooklyn sat in the driver's side of the truck, hands over her face as she cried, her entire body shaking with the sobs.

Throwing the door open, I wrapped my arms around her and said, "It's not what you think. It was a photoshoot. I have no interest in any of those women. It's just a misunderstanding. Please, please let me explain. Please don't leave. Not again. It's just a misunderstanding." The words flew out of my mouth in my hurry to make her understand.

She turned and buried her face against my throat, sobbing still. "I'm sorry. I shouldn't have come without telling you. I shouldn't have—"

"I'm so glad you're here. I'm so happy to see you." I peppered kisses on her hair, pushed her back, and peppered them on her face. "I've missed you so, *so* much."

"I'm so embarrassed," she admitted as she sniffled. "I don't know what came over me. I just saw you with them, and the one put her hand on you, and I—"

"It triggered you," I realized.

She nodded and tucked her head against my neck again.

"It's totally understandable and I'm sorry you had to see that. The shoot setup wasn't even my idea, and I argued with my manager about it, but he still insisted. Since we got home from the vacation, I haven't even left the house, let alone looked at a woman other than you."

Her crying stopped and her sniffling slowed. I rubbed her back with one hand while the other rested on the back of her head, holding her close.

"You have no reason to feel embarrassed. I'm the one who is embarrassed. When I saw you, I thought I was imagining it. Being able to see you and hold you is all I've been thinking about the past three days."

"You're really happy I came? Not just saying that because of what happened?" she stared down at my chest, fidgeting with her hands.

"This is the best surprise I've ever been given," I replied, took the hand off the back of her head, put my fingers beneath her chin, and tilted it up. It was time to be vulnerable and real with her. It was the least I owed her and hopefully it would help ease some of her doubt. "I'm just a beta. I can't growl like an alpha. I can't purr to soothe you. I don't have a knot to fill that need during your heat. I can't claim you by biting you. As a beta, I am not integral to your pack. However, your scent stirs my soul, calls to me in a way I have never experienced before. When I realized I could have my second chance with you, I thanked any and every god or goddess that might exist. Kirk and Buck are my pack and they are my rocks, keeping me steady in the craziness of this world. We butt heads often, but the one thing we agree on wholeheartedly is you. So, please allow me to take you home and show you that I am truly sorry for high school, and for today."

She listened to me without interrupting, which I was grateful for. Though, when I'd started, she looked like she wanted to say something.

After a heavy silence with her staring into my eyes and me panicking about her response, she said, "I'd like to see your home." Her brows furrowed, and she touched my cheek. "Did you run into something?"

Kirk's fist.

"It's just a bruise," I said and pressed my hand over the top of hers. "I really am sorry, Brooklyn."

"I'm sorry I overreacted," she said. "I'll follow you back, since I don't know where I am."

"Can you turn your phone on, just in case we get separated?" I requested.

She blushed and nodded. "Yeah, sorry, I was just overwhelmed with all the calls and messages coming in."

Kirk must have been calling and messaging her as well.

"Let's go, beautiful." I shut the door and climbed into my car. The sooner I got her home, the sooner I could cuddle her.

We drove into the garage and parked. I rushed out and opened her door, immediately pulling her into a hug.

She rubbed her face on my chest. "I'm sorry for running off."

"Promise not to do that again? Promise to talk things out instead?" I requested.

She nodded and set her hands on my chest.

I needed to touch her more, so I picked her up.

She immediately wrapped her legs around my waist and

put her arms around my neck, resting her head against my cheek. "You smell so good," she whispered.

"So do you," I replied. "Now, let's go inside and ease Kirk's fury and worry."

"Fury? Is he mad at me?" Her scent soured slightly in what seemed like anxiety.

I quickly pushed open the door into the kitchen. "No."

Kirk stood at the island, finishing making four plates of dinner. "The photographer said they got enough shots and he'll send them to you and your manager to review in a few days after he works on them."

What probably happened was he growled at them until they left.

Brooklyn tensed around me a moment, exhaled quietly, and tapped me to put her down.

My desire to keep hold of her warred with the knowledge that I should do what she wanted for a brief moment, but I set her down on her feet.

She turned to look at Kirk, her face bright red, and quickly looked down at her clenched hands. "I'm sorry I over-reacted and ran out and … stole your truck."

"Are we good?" Kirk asked. "Did he grovel enough? Do you want me to hold him down so you can punch him a few times? It will make you feel better. It always does me."

She smirked. "Thank you, but no. We're fine." She looked up at me and asked, "Will you give me a tour after we eat?"

So fucking hot. This woman was absolutely stunning.

"I'll do anything you want me to," I said.

Her smile widened. "Don't make promises you won't keep. What if I asked you to do something crazy?"

"Nothing you ask me could be too crazy. The craziest thing I've ever done was think I could live without you and nothing can top that."

She fanned her face while smiling. "Ooh, you are a smooth talker!"

"Go put a shirt on," Kirk ordered me. He carried two of the plates towards the dining room. "Follow me, sweetheart."

Brooklyn pouted. "Are you sure he has to put a shirt on? I'm enjoying the view."

Kirk chuckled. "Come on, we can have naked meals later."

She followed after Kirk with one last look at me.

I gave her a wink and flexed my pecs to make them bounce.

Her feet stopped and she was about to turn, but Kirk called her, making her turn around and jog into the dining room.

Chuckling, I hurried upstairs to my room to change and wash my face, since I had a little bit of makeup on from the photoshoot.

It still didn't seem real that she was here, that she had flown to see us.

Picking out what to wear was suddenly hard, but I reminded myself she wouldn't really care that much about what I was wearing. I went to the safe in my closet, opened it, and pulled out the necklace I had purchased as an apology gift. My original plan had been to mail it to her with a long, heartfelt apology letter. Giving it to her and apologizing in person so I could see her face was a much better option.

I put it in my pocket, not wanting to do it before dinner.

Brooklyn sat at our dining table with her elbows on the table and chin resting on her hands. "The only thing I brought was my work laptop."

"We have spare toothbrushes, and you can wear my shirt to sleep in tonight, since it'll be a dress on you," Kirk offered.

Instead of sitting down right away, I walked around, kissed her cheek, and then took my seat.

"Honey, I'm home!" Buck called as he entered the house. The weirdo loved saying that every time he came home.

"Dining room!" Kirk called out and winked at Brooklyn.

She smoothed her clothes down and fidgeted in her seat. Was she worried about how Buck would react?

"What is that delicious smell?" he said with a slight growl in his voice. "It almost smells like—" He stepped into the room and stopped speaking, his mouth hanging open at the sight of Brooklyn.

"Surprise?" she said and threw her arms out.

Buck ran around the table, scooped her up, and hugged her hard, burying his face against her neck. "Am I dreaming? Is it really you?"

She hugged him back and sucked in a huge breath of his scent. "No, you are not dreaming. Yes, it's really me."

Buck purred and rubbed his cheek against the top of her head. "I missed you."

"Will you guys react this way every time you come home and see me?"

"Yes," all three of us said simultaneously.

Buck finally set her down and took his seat at the table, sitting across from her.

"So, um, now that we're all here, I'd like to officially start our courting." Her cheeks reddened as she finished the sentence. After a brief pause, she added, "If you all still want to accept me."

I'd planned to do it after dinner, but now seemed like the better time. Getting out of my seat, I got onto my knees next to her and held up the necklace box. "Before we discuss courting, please accept this apology gift. I know it is long overdue and I cannot begin to imagine the pain I caused you, but know that I am deeply, deeply sorry. I'm an idiot and although I can't go back in time to fix things, I hope you'll let me use the rest of our lives to make it up to you. You are the only woman for me. I am sorry, Brooklyn. I am so sorry."

She threw her arms around me and tackled me to the ground, rubbing her cheeks along mine. "I forgive you."

I kissed her face and then her lips. "Thank you for giving me another chance."

After one more kiss, she got back into her chair and opened the box. Her eyes widened at the sight of the rose-shaped diamond necklace. "It's gorgeous."

"Everything pales in comparison to you," I said as I put it on her.

She touched it gently and smiled wide. "Smooth talker."

"Since you've accepted our beta's apology, let's get back to the matter of our courting," Buck said. "We have all prepared courting gifts for you, and will give them to you after dinner. Is that acceptable?"

She nodded.

"Great, let's eat!"

Brooklyn

DINNER WAS DELICIOUS, and being back with them filled a hole I hadn't realized had formed.

The necklace and apology from Tyler were great, but when they gave me my courting gifts, I almost fainted.

Buck given me a signed painting by my favorite artist and Tyler had given me a gorgeous diamond bracelet that matched the necklace, but Kirk's was the cherry on this courting present sundae.

"A f-f-first edition?" I gasped as I stared into the box Kirk had given me. It was my favorite book and super hard to find.

"Open the book," Kirk said.

I almost didn't want to touch it, but carefully lifted the front cover. My heart stopped, and I gasped for breath. Signed. It was signed by the author.

"I think she likes it," Tyler teased.

"Breathe, sweetheart," Kirk said with a satisfied smile.

"If I hadn't already agreed to court you all, these would have solidified it," I whispered. "They're amazing."

"We'll put the book and painting in the shared safe to ensure they don't get ruined while you're here," Kirk said.

I set the box down, jumped up, threw my arms around his neck, and kissed him. He put his arm around my back to keep me up. I flicked my tongue against his lips and he opened willingly, his tongue and mine dancing together.

I pulled back, panting, and he reluctantly set me on my feet, letting me go.

"How about that tour?" I asked.

Tyler stood and held out his hand. "You bet."

Linking our hands together, I followed him out of the living room, one of three that they had, and around the rest of the ground floor. Everything was very modern chic in decor and design.

"Did you do the interior design?" I asked as he pushed open the door to his recording studio.

"No, we bought the house like this," Tyler answered. "Thankfully, it will help us sell it easier, too."

In addition to the recording studio, their individual rooms, two spare rooms, and the living rooms I'd seen, they also had a large gym and theater room, and the basement was a huge man cave with a full bar, dartboard, pool table, and eighty-inch TV. There was also a detached building which was Kirk's woodworking.

I stared out the back door, looking at the huge pool and trees that served as the property line, and also blocked people from getting pictures of them easily.

"This place is really amazing," I said, and once again felt bad that they would have to give it up to move to me.

They were making a lot of sacrifices, or compromises, but I wasn't.

Could I move my plans up for the business? Could I implement them now instead of in a year?

"What's wrong?" Buck asked, wrapping his arms around me from behind. He rested his chin on my shoulder and kissed my cheek.

"What if we stayed here?" I whispered. "Would you want to stay here?"

"What do you mean?" he asked, straightened, and turned me around to look at me. "Stay here tonight?"

"No, I mean ... would you want me to move in here instead of you moving to California and buying a new place?"

He frowned. "You can't relocate your business. We told you we were fine moving to you."

"Yes, I know, but would you be fine living here instead? Would you rather stay here than move?"

"I don't know about rather, but if you wanted to move here with us instead, we would be fine with that," he said and brushed a thumb across my cheek. "We want you to be happy and comfortable."

"Okay," I said and exhaled. "I'm not sure if I can make it work, but I think it might be possible. I need some time to figure it all out."

"We're not rushing you," he said and kissed me lightly on the lips. "We'll give you as much time as you need."

I nodded, silently going over what I would need to do to accomplish this.

"Do you want to get changed into something more comfortable?" he asked.

I nodded again. "Yes, please."

Taking my hand, he led me up the stairs to his bedroom. I sat on the end of his bed while he pulled out a pair of pajama pants and tossed them to me.

They were super soft, and I ran my hand across them a few times while humming appreciatively.

"I'll go grab you a shirt from Kirk," he said, and left the room.

Seizing the opportunity, I stripped out of my clothes and lay on my side on the bed, hoping I looked as seductive as I was attempting to.

Buck walked in, looking down at the shirt in his hands. "This was the softest one I could find, so I hope it's okay." He looked up and froze for a breath before immediately tossing the shirt to the side, shutting his door, and marching towards me.

I rolled onto my hands and knees and crawled down the middle of the bed towards him. "I think I'll wait to get dressed."

He nodded, pulled his shirt off, and said, "I think I'll join you."

When I had smelled Kirk at the airport, my slick had increased, and throughout dinner, getting their gifts, and the tour it had become so much that I had soaked through my thong and pants.

As soon as Buck was close enough to touch, I sat up and set my hands on his warm chest. "You have a lot of tattoos," I commented, running my finger along a tribal one that went from his chest to his shoulder. He had a ton more, so many more that his chest and shoulders barely had bare skin showing.

"You like tattoos?" he asked, set his hands on my hips, and rubbed his thumbs over my hip bones.

I nodded. "Very much so."

"Did you know that Buck, Tyler, and I have matching tattoos?" He skimmed his fingers along my sides, barely brushing along the outer edge of my breasts, and went back down before repeating the motion.

I took a shuddering breath and shook my head. "I-I did not."

"Well, maybe the next time we're all together, we'll show you," he said, squatted down, and took my nipple into his mouth.

I moaned and let my head fall back. "S-Sounds like a plan."

His hand slid between my legs where my slick was dripping down the insides and stroked between my folds. "Damn, you're so wet."

Leaning my face down so I could draw in more of his scent, I said, "It's your scents. I soaked through my pants by the time we made it up here. I've ... never had that happen before." Admitting it seemed like a good thing. It was best to be open and honest with each other. Plus, I thought it might make him feel good, increase his ego, to know that it was because of them.

Judging by the bulge in his pants, I was not the only one affected.

"Your scent affects us, too," he admitted. He dipped his

fingers into me, making me moan and tighten around them. I gripped his shoulders to stay upright.

"I want you," I panted. "I need you."

"Good things come to those who wait," he said as he gently pushed me backwards onto my back on the bed.

I pouted at him, which made me smile as he lowered his face down and licked me.

Arching up into his mouth made him chuckle.

He pressed down gently on my stomach, forcing me to remain flat. "Be a good girl and let me do my job."

"Your job?" I asked, and lifted my head to look at him. "You're a professional cunnilingus-er? I think we need to have a talk about your job if we're going to pack up. I'm not sure I like the idea of you doing this with other women."

"It's my job to please you," he explained. "Now, where was I?" He sucked my clit into his mouth and I tried to buck up again, but he kept his hand on my stomach. He held me down as he devoured me, licking, sucking, and making me moan. Intensifying my pleasure, he slid two fingers inside of me, pumping in time to his licks and sucking.

Stars danced across my eyes as I orgasmed harder than I ever had before and screamed his name. Slick squirted out of me.

"I'm sorry," I apologized quickly.

He sat up, face wet, and smiled. "Why are you apologizing? That's exactly what I wanted you to do. Please, drown me in it."

I pointed at his chin. "You've got a little right there."

Laughing, he grabbed a towel from his adjoining bathroom, and wiped his face off. "Did I get it?"

I nodded as I panted on the bed. "That was ... amazing."

"That was just the warm-up," he said as he unbuttoned and unzipped his pants, then slowly slid them off. His erection sprang free, and I licked my lips at the thick, hard length before me.

"Yes, please," I breathed.

Crawling up the bed above me, he slotted himself at my entrance, and asked, "Do you want a condom? Any ground rules?"

"No condom necessary since I'm not in heat," I reminded him. Sure, there was a chance I could get pregnant, but it was really rare.

"Anything else?" he asked and pressed the tip of his head harder against my entrance.

I shook my head vigorously, ready for him to start.

Thankfully, he didn't keep me waiting, pushing into my soaked and aching core.

"Yes," he moaned.

I expected a slow, steady pace, but instead he set a hard, bruising pace that had our skin slapping together so fast and hard someone outside might have thought I was clapping.

Oh, I was definitely clapping at his performance and would likely have liquid legs unable to support me once he finished.

"I'm getting close," I begged, nearly out of my mind from the pleasure. "I want your knot, please."

"Please, what?" he asked, pressing his knot against my entrance, making me stretch a tad, but not pushing hard enough to enter me.

"Please, Alpha," I panted.

He purred. "Oh, I do enjoy hearing you say that, beautiful." He slid almost all of the way out of me, then back in until his knot stretched me open even wider for him. His knot was large, but my body was prepared, biology making me ready for his knot to be inside of me and bind us together.

My orgasm peaked just as his knot fully filled me in the most perfect way. I screamed joyously as stars danced across my eyes.

Buck moaned, and I felt him spurting his release inside of me, which triggered another orgasm from me. The pulse of his knot in me and my own walls pulsing, extended our orgasms until I thought I might pass out from the pleasure.

Propped up on his elbow to keep from squishing me, he smiled down at me. "Are you okay?"

His knot was still swollen inside of me, but slowly started shrinking. It was a strange feeling, but not bad. "Yes, just ... this is the first time I've been knotted." Admitting it had me blushing and embarrassed.

His eyes widened slightly. "You let me knot you for your first time?"

Telling him I hadn't planned it would probably make him feel like I regretted it, which I didn't, so I just nodded.

A huge smile split his face, and he kissed me hard on the lips.

Okay, so that had definitely been the right choice.

"Would you like to shower before getting dressed?" he asked.

I nodded.

Another few seconds and his knot deflated enough to

allow him to pull out of me. It was both a relief and yet a feeling of something missing simultaneously.

So weird.

As I lay contemplating the strange feelings, Buck scooped me up in his arms and carried me to the bathroom.

The bathroom was made up of grey and black tiles, but there were no items or decorations that made me think of Buck.

"Do you guys just not like decorating or adding personal touches to your rooms?" I asked as we waited for the water to get hot.

He looked around his bathroom with a frown. "Well, we only moved in six months ago and I never really thought about adding anything in here. It's a bathroom, you know?"

"You don't even have a face towel or something? I have a monogrammed one. Maybe that's just more of a girly thing to do." I had never really considered it before, but maybe these manly men didn't really do things I considered normal because I wasn't around that type of mentality.

Or maybe I was overthinking it.

"Now that I'm thinking about it, I guess you are right. My dads had little signs with funny football sayings and other things in their bedrooms and bathrooms." He scowled, but then looked at me and smiled. "Want to go shopping with me tomorrow to get some decorations?"

"I'd love to," I agreed with a smile. "Wait, don't you have work?"

He looked a bit sheepish and stepped into the shower. "I took off the next couple of days to spend with you."

"You didn't have to do that," I gasped as I stepped into the shower with him. He moved to the side so I could get under the warm water instead of getting hit by the cold splashes.

After getting my hair wet, Buck started massaging shampoo into it.

"I know I didn't have to, but I want to spend as much time with you as I can. Plus ..." He paused so long I thought he wouldn't finish. "... I was going to be jealous of the others spending more time with you."

My smile was cut short as he pushed my chest, making me go back beneath the water, and water poured down my face.

He laughed, and I wiped water out of my eyes while shaking my head at him.

"So, what's the plan for the rest of the night?" I asked. Once my hair was rinsed, I grabbed the shampoo from him and started working his hair into a lather. At first, I was on my tip toes, but he spread his legs a bit to lower himself.

"Shows, snacks, and cuddling?" he suggested.

Cuddling. I'd always wanted to lay about getting cuddled. Was that my life from now on? Would they cuddle me whenever I wanted?

"Babe?" he asked softly, and touched my cheek.

"I'd like cuddles," I said, and pushed his head under the water to get him back.

CHAPTER 22

Kirk

WAKING up to Brooklyn's scent drifting through the house made my morning wood even harder. Waking up to her next to me, wrapped in my arms, meant I got to act on my desires immediately.

Since Buck had slept with her yesterday, his scent had permeated from her, so I'd stolen her to my bed to cover her in my scent. Putting my seed inside her would make her smell even more like me, which was my next plan.

Kissing my way from her shoulder down to her neck, and up to her lips woke her up.

"Hello," she said groggily with a smile that stole my heart and wiped the sleep from her eyes.

"Hello, beautiful." I resumed kissing my way around her throat and rubbed each of my cheeks against hers.

She reached down and stroked my erection through my boxers. "I know you're not supposed to have dessert before you even have breakfast, but ..." Her cheeks were tinged pink, whether from shyness or desire, I didn't know, but it was fucking hot.

"Who am I to deny an omega's wishes?" I said and immediately claimed her mouth with mine, licking along the seam of her lips to get her to open to me.

She did, without hesitation.

A happy growl rumbled through my chest, and she moaned in response.

Sitting back, I pulled her up into a sitting position, pulled the shirt off over her head, and was rewarded with her beautiful breasts. She hadn't worn a bra to bed.

I pushed her chest, making her lie back down, and bent to swirl my tongue around each perky nipple, at attention for me.

She arched up off the bed, rubbing her lower body against my erection. "Please, Alpha. Don't tease me so early in the morning."

With one quick jerk, the borrowed sweatpants came off with her thong, giving me access to her dripping core. Sliding my fingers between her slit, I looked up at her from beneath my lashes. "I have to make sure you're ready for me first."

She nodded emphatically. "I'm ready."

Pushing two fingers into her, I found that she was indeed ready. Slick poured out of her as I pumped my fingers in, a wet spot already forming on the bed that had my chest swelling with pride.

She threw her head back, arched her lower body up, and screamed my name as she orgasmed.

"Any ground rules?" I asked as I lined up with her

entrance, licking her slick off my fingers one at a time while she watched, licking her own lips.

"No," she breathed. "Knot me, please. Give me your knot, Kirk. I want all of you."

When she had been in heat and told us not to knot her, it had been so hard to resist the urges. Now, I would give in and show her just what she'd missed out on.

Even though she was still dripping, I wasn't small, and I didn't want to hurt her. I took it slow, easing into her, letting her body adjust. Her walls fluttered around me, doing their job in accommodating my size. Once I was fully seated up to my knot, I pulled back out, a moan escaping me. "You feel so fucking good."

She panted and nodded. "You too."

"I think this might be a quick dessert," I told her honestly. "You feel so good."

"Quick and dirty is good," she agreed, nodding again.

Sitting back on my legs, I gripped her hips, arched them up, and hit it hard and fast. As soon as she orgasmed, her slick sprayed between us and splashed across her stomach and mine. Again. I needed to make her do that, again. I wanted to be coated in her slick.

"Flip," I ordered, the word coming out as an unintended alpha bark that had her scurrying onto her hands and knees. She lowered her top half, presenting me with an amazing unobstructed view of her dripping and hungry vagina.

Grabbing her hips, I lined up and slammed into her, knowing she was already prepared, waiting for me.

"Yes!" she screamed and bit the bedsheet.

My knot pulsed, but I didn't want to knot her yet. I wanted her to orgasm more. More of her slick to spray me.

Within seconds, she squirted again, screaming my name as I continued my thrusts.

I reached around and squeezed one of her breasts while the other hand continued to grip her hip, thrusting in and out of her.

"You want my knot, omega?"

She nodded.

"Say it."

"Yes."

"Yes, what?"

"Yes, Alpha. I want your knot."

Pulling out of her, I fell onto my back and patted my thigh. "On top."

She turned around and scrambled up my legs, straddling my hips, and immediately dropped down onto me, spearing herself on my cock.

"Fuck," I moaned as she bounced up and down on me. I grabbed and kneaded both of her breasts, pinching her pink nipples just hard enough to make her gasp and moan.

"Are you ready?" she asked, biting her lower lip between her teeth.

I nodded, unable to speak as I watched the goddess before me ride my dick.

She sat down harder, my knot stretching her, but it wasn't enough. She rose back up and dropped back down, successfully taking all of my knot. "Yes!" she screamed and moved her hips from side to side, drawing out her orgasm even more.

My hands dropped to her hips, gripping them as I joined her, orgasming for the longest I had ever orgasmed before.

She dropped her upper half down, her head resting against my chest, and panted. "Best dessert ever," she whispered.

I laughed and kissed the top of her head. "I agree. I think I've just become a fan of dessert before breakfast."

She looked up and smiled at me, laughing softly.

Perfect. She was absolutely perfect. And she was mine. I wasn't going to let anything take her from me.

After cleaning up, I waited for her to put her clothes from the previous day on before following her downstairs to the kitchen for breakfast.

Tyler already had breakfast cooked and was dishing it out on plates when we entered. He smiled. "Good morning."

Brooklyn skipped around the counter and kissed him on the cheek. "Good morning."

"Would you like milk or orange juice for breakfast?" I asked, and opened the fridge.

"Do we have champagne?" she asked.

Tyler chuckled. "Mimosas on a Thursday?"

"Well, if I am going through a midlife crisis, I better do it right," she said around a piece of bacon she had snagged off the plate and munched happily on.

"I think we do," I said and walked into the pantry where we kept our food and had a section of various alcohol bottles. In the back corner was a single bottle of champagne. I grabbed it and stepped out of the pantry. "We've got one bottle left!"

"Yay!" she squealed and clapped her hands excitedly.

It was the cutest thing I had ever seen.

"Let's carry the plates into the dining room while Kirk makes your drink," Tyler suggested.

She quickly grabbed two plates and walked into the dining room.

Buck walked into the kitchen, scratching his head with his eyes barely open. "Morning."

"Morning. Breakfast is in the dining room." I opened the champagne and was glad it didn't spray everywhere.

"Mimosas?" Buck asked, a brow quirked.

"Our girl's request," I said with a smirk.

He smiled. "Our girl, huh? I love the sound of that. Speaking of that, where is she? I can smell her."

I grabbed one of the champagne flutes we had out of the top cupboard, poured champagne in it, then some orange juice, and tilted my head towards the dining room. "Already in there." Remembering we had strawberries, I grabbed one, washed it, cut it up, and added a few into the drink, plus one on the rim.

"Nice touch," Buck said as he grabbed a glass of milk for himself.

"It's the little things that women appreciate."

He smirked. "Is that why they like Tyler so much?"

"I heard that, asshole!" Tyler said from the dining room.

Buck and I laughed as we walked in, joining them at the table.

I set the glass down in front of Brooklyn, and her eyes widened. "I love strawberries! Thank you." She leaned over and kissed me on the cheek.

"Are you two coming with us this morning?" Buck asked Tyler and me.

"Where are you going?" Tyler asked.

"Yes," I answered immediately. I would go wherever Brooklyn went.

"We're going to get her some clothes and necessities, as well as some decorations for the house," Buck answered, before shoveling a huge bite of eggs into his mouth.

"Decorations?" Tyler asked, looked at me, and raised his eyebrows, clearly confused.

"You guys don't have any decorations or things that show your personality," Brooklyn explained. "Your rooms, living rooms, and even the theater room are super basic. It's like a rich, old man with no personality lives here."

"Did she just call us old?" I asked with a growl.

Brooklyn smirked. "If the shoe fits."

I growled louder at her and she shivered in her seat. "Oh, growl more."

"Only if you say please," Buck growled at her.

"Children, we need to let Brooklyn eat breakfast, or our omega isn't going to last," Tyler chastised us.

Brooklyn froze, fork midway to her mouth when he called her ours. After a shuddering breath, she ate her food and smiled wide while looking down at her plate, a soft blush on her cheeks.

So, she liked hearing it, did she? That was good to know and something I would use later.

"I'm going to stay back and work on a song that's been brewing in my skull. It's haunting even my sleeping hours," Tyler said.

It had been a while since he'd been in a mood like this, which was definitely a good sign.

Glancing at Brooklyn, I immediately knew the reason.

"I guess I should only have one of these if we're going out in public next," she said and pouted at her almost empty mimosa.

Buck stood, grabbed her glass, and said, "One more will be fine since you aren't driving."

My lip lifted as I held back a growl since he had beaten me to refilling her drink.

"Do you need anything while we are out?" I asked Tyler.

He thought about it a moment and shook his head. "No, I think I'm good."

"Text us if you do think of anything," I added.

He nodded, finished his food, kissed Brooklyn on her cheek, and went up to his studio.

"He okay?" she asked after he was gone.

"Yeah. When he gets a song idea in his head, he can't stop until he gets it out and recorded just how he wants it. It's a good thing, actually."

"A good thing?" she asked and set her fork down.

Buck returned with her drink, copying my strawberry addition, and set it down with a kiss on her lips.

She rubbed her face against his before he pulled away and took a big drink.

I growled softly, which made Buck smile widely.

Punk.

"It's a good thing because he hasn't been in that mode in quite a while," I explained. "It means his muse is back. That he's being creative again."

"Oh," she said, her eyes widening.

"Drink your mimosa while we clean up," I told her. I grabbed her plate and mine while Buck grabbed his and Tyler's.

Buck followed me into the kitchen and bumped his shoulder against mine. "So?"

"So, what?" I asked back.

He scraped the food into the trash from his and Tyler's plates and gave me a look. "How was your morning?"

I smiled. "A lady never kisses and tells."

Shaking his head, he laughed at my joke.

"Plus, I'm sure you heard and smelled how it went."

"She smells amazing," he purred.

I nodded my agreement, grabbed the dish brush, and cleaned off the plates before putting them in the dishwasher.

"Divine," I said.

A thought occurred to me, and I spun to look at him. "Why are you here? Aren't you supposed to be at work?"

"Like I was going to be able to focus on work when she's here." He shook his head. "I took a couple days off so I could be with her."

"There goes my plan," I said with a dramatic sigh.

He pushed his shoulder against mine and laughed softly.

I bumped him back and joined his laughter.

"All done," Brooklyn said, sauntered up to the sink between us, and rinsed her glass out.

The small woman stood between us, and an intense sense of rightness filled me.

This was where she was supposed to be. This was where I wanted her to stay.

Forever.

My teeth ached to claim her in that exact instant. I wanted to bite down and mark her permanently.

"Kirk?" she asked softly, brows furrowed as she looked up at me with worry.

I spun away and clenched my hands into fists. "Shoes," I said like that explained everything.

CHAPTER 23

Brooklyn

Neither Kirk nor Buck would explain what had caused Kirk's strange reaction to me rinsing my glass.

Had he been upset that I'd finished my drink so quickly? Or that I'd pushed between him and Buck? Or maybe that I cleaned the glass myself?

There were so many possible answers, but I hesitated to ask the question.

Buck drove us in his SUV, letting me sit in the passenger seat while Kirk took the back.

Buck glanced at Kirk several times in the rearview mirror on the drive, but no one spoke the entire drive to the little strip mall they chose.

"I'll make it quick," I whispered as I climbed out of the SUV before either could get out and open my door for me.

The home goods store before me was a popular chain one, so I knew I would be able to find most of the things I needed here.

"Bro, what the fuck?" Buck hissed at Kirk behind me.

"Sorry, I'm good now. Sorry," Kirk apologized.

"Don't apologize to me. She's stressed out and anxious now. Fix it." Buck growled and hurried to catch up to me.

Acting like I hadn't heard them, I walked into the store and down the first aisle.

"Do you want a cart or just a basket?" Buck asked.

I shrugged. "Either is fine." Stopping, I grabbed a toothbrush and the brand of toothpaste I liked.

Kirk held out a basket. "You can put them in here and I'll carry the basket for you."

"Thanks," I said and ducked my head after putting the two items inside.

Kirk growled, making the hair on my nape stand to attention. "Brooklyn, I'm sorry if I upset you. I—"

"Upset me?" I asked, and spun to look up at him. "I'm the one who upset you. I just don't know how. What did I do? Was it the drink, or coming between you and Buck, or cleaning the glass or—"

He grabbed my face between his massive hands and kissed me gently on the lips. "Deep breath, baby girl."

I obeyed, took a deep breath and let it out slowly.

"You didn't upset me or do anything wrong. I just really enjoyed seeing you with us at the sink, like a pack. It felt ... good."

Oh. Oh!

"You promise I didn't upset you?"

He smooshed my cheeks together as I asked, making my lips go wonky and the words come out weird at the end. "Yes, I promise." He kissed me again. "No more worrying. Okay?"

I nodded as much as I could while he continued to squish my cheeks.

He kissed me again and growled before quickly releasing me and stepping back. "You're gorgeous, and if I don't stop now, I'm going to take you right here in the corner of this store."

"Tease," I breathed as I stepped away from him and resumed my shopping, but this time with a smile on my face.

Twenty minutes later, I'd gathered the toiletries I needed and a few other things. I moved to the other side of the store to look through the blankets. The guys had some blankets, but I loved to sit on the couch with a super soft fleece blanket while watching TV and they didn't have one.

As I felt a few of the blankets, trying to decide which to get, out of the corner of my eye, I spotted a nesting canopy. It was a canopy that you put over your bed to make it feel more closed in, more like a nest, something omegas craved during our heats. My heat wasn't happening anytime soon, so I turned away from it and back towards the blankets.

"Can't decide on which color to get?" Buck asked, coming to my side to feel a few of them, too.

"Yeah, I like these two blankets, but can't decide if I like the blue or green better," I admitted.

He grabbed both and put them in a shopping cart I hadn't seen him grab. "We'll get both. Actually..." He reached back and grabbed another of each color, so we had four now. "I think it'd be better if we had one for each male to put our scents on and a spare or one for you if you want it."

"Okay," I agreed with a smile.

Heading down the next rows, which had bathroom decorations and accessories, I stopped next to one and picked it up. It was a hand towel with an embroidered rose and said, "Our Precious Omega."

Normally, I rolled my eyes at things like that, but now I sort of ... wanted it.

I realized Buck was watching me, so I quickly moved over, grabbing a towel near it that had a music note embroidered on it. "I'm going to get this for Tyler."

Kirk walked behind us, pushing the cart, and I realized he had way more things in it than I'd picked.

"What are—"

"Come on, there's lots more to get," Buck said, turning me back around before I could look at the items in the car too long.

"Alright, keep your secrets," I teased.

I found a few more decorations as we walked around the store, including some pillows for the couch with silly phrasing on them.

The last area of the store was full of nesting supplies. I gnawed anxiously on my lip as I walked by them, glancing longingly, but it wasn't time for that. Nesting supplies could be purchased when we finally decided on where we were living.

"Anything else?" Kirk asked.

I shook my head. "That's everything from here."

Buck put his arm around my shoulders and guided me towards the exit. "Great. Kirk will purchase those, and you and I can head to the next store to start our shopping there."

"Secrets are bad," I said and gave him and pouty lip.

He tapped my lower lip and shook his head. "We aren't

keeping secrets, gorgeous. We're preparing surprises. Much different."

"Mmhmm," I said, but couldn't stop the smile from forming.

The next store was a woman's clothing store. I grabbed clothes in my size off the racks, piling my arms up, but Buck took them from me.

"Don't you feel ... emasculated to follow me around carrying things for me?" I asked softly.

Several women in the store giggled and looked at Buck. I resisted the urge to hiss at them and tell them he was mine. Sure, we weren't mated yet, but we were courting and they could back off. I knew he was hot, but dammit.

"No, I am quite enjoying myself," he answered. "I've always wanted a woman to dote on and do things for. Plus, it's not like you threw the clothes at me and demanded I hold them. I offered."

"So, if I did this, would it change your mind?" I grabbed a dress off the rack and tossed it at him, smiling widely.

He caught it and added it to his pile. "It'll only upset me if you don't let me see how good it looks on my bedroom floor."

Heat rushed to my core, and slick pooled.

Buck tensed, as he must have smelled my arousal.

"Tease," I breathed and hurried to gather more items instead of facing him.

Just as we headed to the changing rooms, Kirk rejoined us.

"Awesome," he said and sat in one of the chairs. "I arrived just in time for the fashion show."

I laughed and walked into the room. "Only if you behave, sirs."

"I don't think I've behaved a day in my life," Buck argued. "Why start now?"

"I behaved way too much, so I'm due for some discord," Kirk said.

I peeked my head out and narrowed my eyes at them. "If you don't behave, the fashion show will end."

They sat up straighter.

"Best behavior," Kirk promised, and Buck nodded his agreement.

I nodded once, satisfied with their answer, and tried on one of the jeans and t-shirt outfits I'd found. The shirt was a little tight in the chest, but when I stepped out to show the guys, they seemed to like it.

"Yes," Buck growled.

Kirk just nodded.

Were they really that excited by jeans and a t-shirt?

Testing things, I put on one of the two dresses I'd grabbed, this one form fitting, strapless, bright pink, short in the front and long in the back. It was definitely for parties or something, not every day, but it was gorgeous. I was honestly surprised this store had a dress this fancy, but I wasn't going to worry about that too much.

When I stepped out of the dressing room, both men stared at me with wide eyes before the look quickly morphed into hunger.

"By your silence, I take it this is a definite no, and I should put it back on the rack?" I asked, spinning on my heel so they couldn't see the huge smile on my face.

"You're getting that dress," Kirk growled. "It's perfect."

"I don't have anywhere to wear it," I said, still facing into the dressing room, so I could hide the huge smile.

"We will find a place for you to wear it," Buck said.

My laughter finally bubbled out, and I closed the door so I could change into one of the other outfits. "Well, if you insist."

"We do. We really do," Buck said.

It took me an hour to get through all the stuff I'd grabbed, and the guys insisted on me getting almost all of it. Clothing chosen, I moved on to undergarments.

Once Buck and Kirk learned what size I was, they separated from me and started picking out lingerie sets.

I left them to their devices with a smile.

Whatever they bought me, I would gladly wear it.

After finding an underwire bra, some thongs, a pack of boy shorts, and a sports bra, I grabbed a few cute pajama outfits. Honestly, if they were anything like the alphas my sisters and friends ended up with, I'd only be wearing their clothes or nothing at all during this courtship.

I was okay with that plan, but it would be good to have these things for when I was dressed. I'd worn a dress without a bra or padding, and had been a bit embarrassed with my headlights on for everyone to see.

My final items were thick, fluffy socks, since my feet were always cold.

Kirk and Buck returned with happy smiles and a cart overflowing.

"Are you guys ready?" I asked.

They nodded.

"Did you find everything you needed?" Kirk asked.

I nodded and tossed the things in my hands into the cart. "Yes, sir."

"Is there anything else you need or want?" Buck asked, and slung his arm around my shoulders as we headed towards the checkout.

"I don't think so, but I wanted to go to the next store for some more decorations. They usually have more things with funny sayings on them."

"Well, this time I'll take you on ahead while Buck pays," Kirk said, and pulled me out from under Buck's arm.

Buck growled, but took the cart and pushed it to the register.

Kirk draped his arm across my shoulders and tugged me against his side. "Is this ... okay?"

I looked up at him with a frown, confused. "Your arm around me?"

He nodded.

I leaned against his side and smiled. "Yes."

The quietest purr came from him, but quickly stopped. "Good."

Once inside the store, I didn't want to separate from Kirk, so I walked slower than I normally would, and ensured he stayed at my side.

I found a few things to put in the kitchen and bathrooms, including a sign that said, "Life is short. Lick the bowl."

A few other items I grabbed included chopsticks, a few large ramen bowls, and a potato bag for microwaving potatoes.

Kirk seemed skeptical of the bag, but I would show him later how amazing it really was.

We checked out just as Buck came in.

"Done already?" he asked.

"Yep," I said with a smile. "Now, can we get some food?" I set a hand on my stomach. "I'm starving."

"Her stomach was growling for the last few minutes, but I could tell she was almost done shopping, so I didn't push it," Kirk explained.

Buck and Kirk carried the bags while we walked out to the SUV.

"What kind of food are you in the mood for?" Kirk asked.

"Cheeseburger, fries, and a milkshake," I replied immediately. "Oh, and after we eat, can we stop by the grocery store?"

"Sure," Buck agreed, and climbed into the driver's seat.

Today was shaping up to be an awesome and fun day.

They took me to a local restaurant where they were clearly regulars.

The waitress skipped over and smiled at Buck. "Hey, handsome! Welcome back in. Do you want your usual?"

"Hello, Anna. Yes, the usual for me and Kirk. Brooklyn, what would you like?" he turned to me with a smile.

Her eyes widened as she looked at me in the corner of the booth, clearly not having seen me.

"I'll have a bleu cheese burger with thin fries and a strawberry milkshake, please," I ordered.

She nodded and almost ran back to the back area, immediately whispering to other female servers there.

"Looks like you guys have a fan club here," I teased.

"It happens," Buck said with a shrug. "I coach some of their kids, too."

"I'm sure their mates just love seeing their goo-goo eyes as they watch you."

"Goo-Goo eyes?" Kirk asked with a frown.

"Like this," I said, and gave them my best expression of longing while watching a male waiter serve food near us.

Kirk and Buck growled.

I laughed and shook my head. "You two are so silly. I was just showing you what the other men see."

"No wonder they always puff up around me," Buck said. "I know some are intimidated by me, but I don't raise my voice often, and I tone down my alpha aura for coaching. Yet, the dads always seemed to act agitated."

"Now you know it's because their mates are sighing over what could have been, if only your scents had matched." I shrugged. "I've been in their shoes a time or two."

That made Kirk growl again.

"Here are your drinks," Ana said. She looked at me and asked, "Are you a relative visiting?"

What a very polite way to ask what my intentions were.

"No, I'm courting these studs," I said with a smile.

Her eyes widened and then she gasped. "You're that woman they rescued! I knew you looked familiar."

A brief bit of panic flared as the memories hit me, but I squashed it. "Yes, that's me."

Buck set his hand on my thigh and rubbed his thumb across the top.

Kirk set his hand on the top of the table and I set mine in it, letting him squeeze it to provide me reassurance.

She took a step back. "Um, well, I'll go check on your order. Glad you're okay."

Once she was gone, I said, "It's okay, guys. I'm fine."

"We won't let anything happen to you," Buck said and nuzzled behind my ear.

"I'm still really impressed that you shot some of them," Kirk said.

"Let's talk about something else," I requested and swallowed hard.

"What do you want to do for dinner tonight?" Kirk asked.

"Actually, I wanted to cook you guys something," I admitted. "Part of the reason I wanted to stop at the grocery store was for a few items I noticed you didn't have."

"You want to cook us something?" Kirk asked with a frown.

"Courting is about showing each other what life could be like, what we have to offer," I reminded him. "I'm not going to let you guys do everything for me. That's not how a partnership works."

Kirk still didn't look convinced, but he didn't say anything else.

My milkshake came out, and I took my time enjoying it. Sweet, strawberry goodness.

"It's been so long since I've had a milkshake," I told them, since they were looking at me strangely.

"Why?" Buck asked.

"Trying to keep my slim figure on the chance that I met potential suitors," I said with a smile.

"You shouldn't deprive yourself of something for men," Kirk said.

I rolled my eyes. "Easy for you to say, big guy. You just growl and it makes women's knees weak."

He smirked. "Oh, is that so?"

Crap. "No, I take it back. That was a lie."

Buck laughed softly and shook his head.

"Don't shake your head. You know it's true for you, too." I took a big spoonful of milkshake and swished it around in my mouth to keep from saying more.

"So, what I'm hearing is that you like our growls?" Buck said in a deeper voice, then stuck his nose behind my ear, and growled softly.

My entire body shivered and slick pooled. "If you don't want to get us arrested for indecent exposure in this restaurant, you should stop."

Both men laughed while I fanned my now hot face.

Our food came out, giving me a reprieve from embarrassing myself any further.

CHAPTER 24

Tyler

THE THREE OF them returned just as I finished uploading the new song and preparing my social media posts.

I hurried down the stairs and out to the garage to help them carry in whatever they'd purchased. And to see Brooklyn, since we had been apart for so many hours.

My eyes nearly bulged out of my head when I saw the number of bags in the back of the SUV.

"It's not my fault," Brooklyn said immediately, her cheeks tinted pink. "They bought things I said I didn't need, and kept convincing me to add more things to the carts as we went."

I hugged her and inhaled her scent; the smell immediately calmed me. "That's a lot of groceries," I commented. I didn't really care about the house stuff and items for her. I'd buy her an entire store if she wanted it.

"I'm going to make you all dinner tonight, and wanted to get some of my favorite snacks and things while I'm staying here," she explained, her face more red than pink now.

"Did you have fun?" I asked as I grabbed several plastic bags by their handles.

She nodded her head vigorously and smiled wide. "I did."

"That's all that matters then," I said and carried the load inside.

Kirk gave her only a couple of bags and shooed her inside to start putting them away in her room. I stayed, watching him because he was acting sketchy. He gave a few bags to Buck, whispering to him too low for me to hear. My assumption was proven right as he grabbed a few bags and took them up to the other spare room, the one we had pre-assigned as our nesting room.

"What did you get?" I asked.

He growled as he spun around and I mentally patted myself on the back for sneaking up on him. "Shut the door," he barked.

I shut it and walked to the bed, where he pulled out several items, including a nesting canopy for the bed.

"She kept looking at it, but walked away from it without adding it to the cart. So, I snuck behind her and grabbed it. I figured if we—"

"If we show her what her nest could look like, it might entice her to stay and accept us," I finished for him. "Good thinking, man."

He smiled. "I also bought her a few other nesting things, because she skipped over the nesting corner. I think she was trying not to scare us, or trying not to get her hopes up or something."

That sounded like Brooklyn.

"I'm glad you grabbed them." If my assumption was right,

she hadn't grabbed them, because grabbing them, setting up a nest here, and then losing it because she still wasn't convinced we were her pack, would hurt her a lot.

The thought of her setting up a nest here and not staying hurt and made me anxious.

"You okay?" Kirk asked, sensing the shift of my feelings, and set a hand on my shoulder.

"Just thinking how much it would hurt to set up a nest, to ultimately have her leave," I admitted. "I think that might be what she was thinking with not buying nesting items."

Kirk tensed as he thought about it. "You might be right. Maybe it would be better if I didn't show her the nesting room until we've convinced her or almost convinced her to accept us."

I nodded my agreement. "I don't want to hurt her unnecessarily, or by accident."

He nodded back.

"Do you know what she's making for dinner?" I asked as we left the room and headed downstairs to help unpack the things they'd purchased.

He shook his head. "Something with beef and potatoes."

"We all love beef and potatoes in their various forms, so that's exciting."

And now I was hungry.

"How'd your song writing go?" Kirk asked.

"I recorded it, and it'll post in the next hour," I admitted with a wide smile.

Kirk's eyebrows shot up into his hairline, and he hugged me hard. "That's awesome, man." He patted my back and smiled wide. "I'm so glad."

"My manager is excited, too," I said with a soft laugh.

They were constantly asking me to post more songs, even if they were just covers, to revitalize my followers. I didn't want to do that, though. I didn't want to be one of those singers who only did covers. Not that there was anything wrong with that, but I wanted to share my songs, the ones I'd written.

"I also wrote about half of another song," I said as we walked into the living room where Brooklyn and Buck were cutting tags off of pillows.

"You wrote a song today while we were shopping?" Brooklyn asked and looked up at me.

She was one of the prettiest women I knew, and having her scent in my house made me stand a little straighter. "Yeah," I finally answered.

"Wow, that's awesome. I could barely decide on towels, and you wrote a song. I feel like an underachiever." She stood and walked over to me with a sheepish smile. "I got you this."

She held out a hand towel with a music note on it. "You picked this out for me?"

She looked at the ground and nodded. "For your bathroom, since you only had a big towel on your counter. I mean, if you prefer the big towel you don't have—"

I hugged her and kissed her cheek. "I love it, thank you."

Looking up, she gave me a bright smile. "You're welcome."

Helping take off tags and open the other items, the four of us made quick work of it. We split up to place the new decorations, and immediately the house felt warmer.

How could simple things like pillows with sayings we

found funny make a house feel warmer and more like a home?

We all offered to help Brooklyn cook dinner, but she forced us out of the kitchen with a wooden spatula.

"Don't come back in here until I'm done," she ordered us with the most adorable growl I'd ever heard.

"How can a growl make me so hard?" Kirk said as he adjusted his pants.

Buck and I laughed, but we weren't unaffected.

"Any issues today?" I asked. The three of us sat in the living room, watching the latest football news.

Both shook their heads.

"Here you go," Brooklyn said, startling me, since I hadn't heard her soft feet enter the room. She set three glasses on the table. Each had ice, a dark liquor of some kind, an orange slice, and a cherry. "My famous Old Fashioneds," she said proudly. "Enjoy while you wait."

Without waiting for our responses, she spun and skipped off to the kitchen again.

Kirk picked his up, sniffed it, and took a drink. His eyes widened. "This is delicious."

Buck and I took drinks of ours and nodded our agreement.

Buck kicked his feet up on the coffee table and leaned back on the couch with his glass in his hand. "I could get used to this."

I laughed and said, "We all could."

"What happens if your music starts blowing up again?" Kirk asked me. "Are you going to go on tour?"

His fear was a valid one, but ...

I shook my head. "No. I won't be going on tour ever again. However, I might be willing to do some shows here. Or, maybe a show or two in Vegas, where we could all go together. The only way I'm leaving the state is if we're all going together."

The scent of the meat cooking had me sniffing loudly. "Whatever she's making smells delicious."

Buck and Kirk nodded.

"Even if it's awful, I'm going to enjoy it," Kirk said.

"Well, anything tastes better than military rations," I said with a shrug.

He and Buck laughed and I felt a tension I hadn't realized was still between us release.

CHAPTER 25

Brooklyn

I HADN'T MEANT to eavesdrop, but I was going to bring them some appetizers when I heard Tyler. What did he mean, "The only way I'm leaving the state is if we're all going together,"? Was one of them considering not moving?

My plan to stay here was accomplishable. Should I tell them that?

Should I admit that I had found a way to stay here with them, instead of forcing them to move to me?

I closed my eyes and shook my head to clear it of all these thoughts. Tonight was the night to show them that I was a good match for them. That I could bring more to the table than a pretty face and ovaries.

Plastering a smile on and thinking of only positive things, I walked into the living room and set the chips and cream cheese with salsa on the coffee table. "I figured you boys would be hungry now, and dinner won't be ready for about an hour. So, I made this real quick."

"Thank you," Tyler said and immediately grabbed a chip.

"You sure you don't need any help?" Kirk asked, looking at me and trying to sniff discreetly.

Could he smell my worry?

"I'm good, thank you. You guys enjoy your television and snack. Just holler if you need a drink refill." I spun back around and hurried to continue making dinner.

Time flew by as I prepared the meal for them, and when I had it finished and plated, a huge smile wouldn't stop forming.

I carried the plates to the dining room and set them on the table, then made us all new drinks that I set at each place setting as well. "Dinner is ready!" I called out and waited in the dining room.

They came in and each of their eyes widened.

"This looks and smells delicious," Buck praised and kissed my cheek before he sat.

"I can't remember the last time I had Shepard's pie," Kirk said softly as he took his seat.

Tyler kissed my cheek and sat down.

"Do you need anything else before we eat?" I asked.

They all shook their heads.

"Sit, eat with us," Kirk requested.

I sat down and everyone dug in.

"Oh my god, it's amazing," Tyler said. He looked at me and added, "Great job."

Try as I might, I couldn't help preening a bit from their praising. The meal was simple, but it still took time and I had a few tricks up my sleeve for making it taste better.

"I don't think I've had it without carrots before," Kirk said.

I flinched a bit. "Um, I don't really like cooked carrots, so I didn't put them in. If you guys prefer them, next time I make it I will add them." I'd just take them out from my own serving.

"No, I like it this way too," he said quickly.

Buck frowned as he took some of the beef and ate it. "What did you put on the meat? It tastes a lot better than the recipe my mom uses."

"That's a secret," I said with a wink. "Oh, I also made dessert. So, don't fill up too much."

"I'm going to gain twenty pounds this week if you keep cooking like this for us," Buck said with a smile as he took another big bite of his food.

"I keep telling you that you need to get back to working out with me," Kirk teased.

"Do you guys usually cook meals or go out to eat?" I asked, curious what their normal nights were like.

"We cook at home about four nights a week, switching off who cooks," Kirk answered. "The other nights we go out, or eat frozen pizza or something. Depends on how lazy we're feeling, or if we don't feel like going out around people."

"I totally understand that," I agreed and then realized something. "I didn't wear my mask today."

"What?" all three asked simultaneously.

My cheeks heated, but I decided to tell them despite the embarrassment. "I have a mask that I wear when I go out in public places, because often, people smell really bad. I didn't have it on today and didn't notice the smell of other people. Is it because you guys were close to me and your scents blocked out the others? Or was I just focused on your scent, so I ignored theirs? I've never experienced that before. I don't remember focusing on your scents. It wasn't a conscious thing."

Kirk and Buck frowned as they looked at each other.

"Now that you mention it, I didn't really notice other peoples' scents either," Kirk said.

"Me neither," Buck said.

"Interesting," Tyler said and tapped a finger against his chin.

"Well, I guess I should say thank you." I smiled at Buck and Kirk. "I hated wearing that mask and the looks people gave me when I did wear it."

We finished our dinner in silence as we all got lost in various thoughts. Whatever the reason, I really was glad that I hadn't worn the mask today.

Maybe this was yet another sign that I really was supposed to be with this pack. A sign that try as I might, I knew I would not be able to ignore.

And really, did I want to ignore it? I enjoyed my time with them, and I was excited to see what the rest of the week had in store for us.

"We'll clear the table, since you made dinner," Kirk said and stood, reaching over and taking my plate before I could pick it up.

"Okay, that will give me time to get your dessert ready for each of you." I skipped ahead of him and pulled the secret dessert I'd baked out of the oven, where it was kept warm until time to eat.

Sneaking glances back to ensure they weren't watching me, I divvied out the dessert and carried it out to the living room. Since they were taking a little longer, I grabbed the TV remote and turned it to the comedy channel. My favorite show was on, one that shared ridiculous videos they found on the internet.

I laughed as I watched someone lose their shoe down a hill of snow.

"I love this show!" Tyler exclaimed as he joined me. He picked up one of the plates and scrutinized it. "What is this?"

"Dessert," I said and laughed as someone kicked a tree, so their friend had snow fall on them.

Tyler took a tentative bite and his eyes widened. "Holy shizz, these are delicious! I still have no idea what it is, but it is yummy."

I shook my head at him, but smiled wider. "I'm glad you like it."

"No, not like ... love." He reached for another plate, but Kirk walked in at that time and smacked his hand.

"No stealing," Kirk growled and sat down on my other side. "Thank you again for dinner and for dessert."

"Don't thank me for dessert until you try it," I said.

"Please don't like it and give it to me," Tyler said as he finished his plate.

"Let's see if I agree with Tyler," Buck said, and sat beside Tyler, grabbing the last plate.

Buck and Kirk took one bite, their eyes widened, and within a minute their plates were empty.

"Um, I take it you liked it? Or, did you hate it so much that you ate it as fast as possible, so you wouldn't hurt my feelings?"

"Is there more?" Kirk asked.

Laughing, I nodded. "In the oven."

"Okay, we need this recipe written down and placed on the fridge, so we can make it all the time," Buck said and pushed Kirk back to try to get off of the couch first.

The trio wrestled with each other as they grappled for getting to the kitchen first.

While they fought, I watched the show. It had been so long since I'd just enjoyed funny videos or shows. It was nice.

"Okay, come on, you have to tell us what this is made out of," Buck begged.

"The main ingredient is saltine crackers," I admitted.

All three turned and stared at me.

"You're lying," Kirk accused me.

I snickered. "Turn it over."

They all did, and Kirk even licked the center that didn't have the topping on it.

"Whoa. Are you a witch?" Tyler asked. "I'm totally cool with it if you are, just wondering."

Laughter exploded out of me, and I held my stomach as tears leaked out of my eyes. "It's a super simple recipe! And one of the few I can make, since I suck at baking."

"This delicious dessert suggests otherwise," Buck whispered and took another bite.

"So, what's the plan for tomorrow?" I asked.

All three shrugged.

Kirk said, "We don't really have any plans yet since..."

Since I'd surprised them by randomly showing up.

"We can figure it out tomorrow, go with the flow," Tyler suggested, and put his arm around me, pulling me against his side.

Kirk set his hand on my leg and I laced our fingers together.

This, this was what I had craved. Me, sitting with my pack and enjoying our time together, even if it was something as simple as watching silly videos.

More. I wanted more. I knew what my nose had tried to tell me now. Courting was pointless. These were my mates, my pack. Fate put us back together, and I didn't want to be separated again.

"Oh no!" Tyler gasped as he looked at his phone. He looked up at Kirk with fear in his eyes. "Tomorrow is the dinner."

"Dinner?" I asked. Why was that scary?

"Fuck," Kirk said, and let his head drop back. "If we try to cancel, they'll just find us."

"What are you guys talking about?" I asked.

"I'm not sure why you two are stressing about it. It's the perfect opportunity for us to introduce Brooklyn to them," Buck said. He leaned around Tyler so I could see him and said, "Tomorrow is dinner with all of our parents."

"That's the issue, all of them at once, and we are only courting her," Tyler said with a groan. "My mom especially is going to bombard Brooklyn if she gets the chance."

"Why don't you want me to meet your families until we confirm our bond?" I asked. "Are you afraid they'll talk you out of it?"

"No!" Tyler shouted and waved his hands back and forth.

"That's not it at all," Kirk said quickly.

"We're worried they're going to overwhelm you and try to pressure you into accepting," Buck said.

Now was as good of a time as any, and the sooner I did this, the better for all of us.

"Oh, well that won't be a problem at all," I said with a wide smile and snuggled into Tyler's side.

"It won't?" Kirk asked softly, cautiously.

"Nope, because I've already decided to accept."

Tyler tensed at my side, not even breathing. I could see Kirk had stilled as well.

"You ... can you say that again?" Buck whispered.

I jumped up to my feet, turned, and smiled at the trio. "I would like to officially accept the three of you as my pack. If that's okay with you?"

Tyler, Kirk, and Buck reached out to me and pulled me down onto the couch, into Tyler's lap, so they could all hug and kiss me.

"Is that a yes?" I asked and laughed.

"Yes, a million times," Tyler said.

"Fuck yes," Kirk said, and kissed my cheek.

"Yes, yes, yes," Buck said.

"So, how about we go upstairs and solidify things?" I suggested.

Tyler picked me up and carried me up the stairs and into a bedroom I hadn't seen.

A gasp escaped as I looked at the bed with a nesting canopy around it. "You bought it?"

Kirk stepped forward, so I could see him, and nodded. "We saw you looking at it and bought it, plus a few other nesting items you avoided."

"We hadn't shown you because we were worried it might upset you," Buck admitted.

"If you want to change this for a different one, we can," Tyler said, and set me down on my feet.

Walking forward, I stroked a hand down the silky material as tears leaked out of my eyes. "Thank you." If I hadn't been certain before, I would be now.

"It's easy to remove, so if we move, we can take it with us," Kirk added quickly.

I turned around and shook my head. "You won't have to move. I've decided to move here, with you."

"Really?" Buck asked, and took a step closer to me.

"It's going to take me a little bit of final work, but I can move here with you."

Kirk stepped forward and crushed his mouth against mine, our tongues meeting immediately as if we were both starving for this connection.

I pulled my shirt off and tugged at his. "Skin," I ordered. "I need skin."

All three took their shirts off immediately.

My bra was being a pain, but Kirk reached around and with a snap of his fingers, unclasped my bra.

"Well, that was impressive." I chuckled.

"Not nearly as impressive as those," Kirk growled and gently cupped my breast with a hand before sucking my nipple into his mouth.

"Yes!" I gasped and arched into him.

Buck tugged my pants off, nudged my legs to spread them wider, dropped to his knees, and sucked my clit into his mouth.

Words escaped me and I just moaned.

Tyler stepped forward, completely naked and stroking

himself. He turned my face gently and kissed me. I reached down and took over stroking him, so hard and yet his skin so soft at the same time.

Kirk switched to the other nipple and after a few more licks and sucks from Buck, I came undone. My screams were swallowed by Tyler and they held me in place, forcing me to ride out the orgasm longer than I would have normally, and keeping me upright when my legs wanted to give ou.

Tyler broke our kiss, but stayed at my side. "I never thought I'd enjoy a woman screaming into my mouth before."

Kirk released my nipple with a pop and pulled his pants down. "I want to try that next time."

Buck stood, wiping his mouth with the back of his arm, and smiled. "Good thing we've got acreage or we might have to warn the neighbors to ignore the screams." He removed his pants and I licked my lips.

"My turn," I said, bent over at the waist, grabbed his leg, and pulled him close enough I could suck the tip into my mouth.

"Oh, fuck," he breathed.

Kirk stepped behind me and pushed at my entrance. "Let's see if you're ready or if we need to up the foreplay."

Oh, I was definitely ready. Normally, I would require more foreplay, but my slick flowed so quick that it slid down my legs to the floor.

He pushed inside gently, taking his time going out and further in each time until he was up to his knot. "Yes, there we go."

Buck moved closer, so I could swallow his thick cock easier. With slow and steady movement, I swallowed him all the way to his knot and flicked my tongue out across the bottom of his knot.

"Fuck," he gasped and his head dropped back as he gripped his thighs to keep from gripping me.

Kirk increased his speed, now that I was stretched enough to accommodate him, and gripped my hips. "God, she feels amazing." His grip tightened even more and the sound of our skin slapping together almost made me come right there.

Tyler reached down and squeezed and stroked one of my nipples, amping me up even more.

Increasing how quickly I went down on Buck and stroked Tyler, my mind and body were on overload. With two more strokes, I come, spraying Kirk and causing slick to drip down his legs.

Euphoric bliss filled me as I had one of the best orgasms of my life.

"Let her up for a second," Kirk ordered Buck as he halted his movements.

Buck stepped back, forcing me to release him from my mouth, and Tyler helped push my upper body upwards so I stood.

Kirk, still buried inside of me, asked, "You ready for me?"

"Pretty sure you're already inside of me, so ..."

He pressed deeper into me, his knot forcing me wider than I already was. "You ready for me?" he asked again.

I panted and nodded vigorously. "Yes."

"Yes, what?" he teased, pulled out a bit, and pressed his knot deeper, but still not all the way in.

"Yes, Alpha!" I yelled, knowing exactly the phrase the egotistical man wanted to hear.

He purred, slid his arm around my stomach and up between my breasts, and slid his knot all the way inside of me.

I cried out in pleasure, but that pleasure was immediately doubled when he bit into my neck, claiming me.

The connection was instant, and I came again.

His knot swelled more, preventing me from moving, and he filled me as he joined me with his own orgasm.

He continued to hold me against him as our bodies were inseparable, thanks to his knot holding me in place. "You're mine now, Brooklyn. I'm never letting you get away ever again."

"Promises, promises," I panted, a huge smile on my face. It was a good thing he held me because my legs were a bit wobbly.

After a few more moments—or minutes, time seemed out of whack for me—his knot deflated enough for him to pull out. He kissed the spot on my neck he had marked, kissed my cheek, and went to the adjoining bathroom to clean up.

Tyler turned me and pushed me gently down onto the bed. "My turn." He didn't give me time to even suggest I clean up before pushing into me in a single stroke that had my head thrown back.

"Yes!" I screamed and raised my hips to meet each of his thrusts.

He raised one of my legs up, using a different angle to hit that perfect spot that had me coming and screaming his name.

Buck crawled on the bed on his knees, presenting me with a perfect angle to suck him all the way down into my throat and to his knot. He reached down and stroked my clit while Tyler continued to pump into me all the way until our bodies slapped together.

Tyler pushed Buck back, fell forward, and bit right above my left breast. Although he couldn't mark me the way an alpha could, he could give me a permanent mark to remind us both of our commitment to each other.

He pulled out of me, gasping for breath. "I'm going to have to join Buck at the gym. My stamina is way too low."

Buck laughed as he took Tyler's place, stroking himself for me to see. "Two down, one to go."

I licked my lips and swallowed hard.

He rubbed the head against my swollen clit, making me gasp and arch up, but he pushed my pelvis down with his hand. "No, I want to make you come before I go back inside of you."

Since I'd already squirted once, I didn't think my clit would be ready to again. I was completely wrong.

Maybe his head was magical or maybe I was just high on orgasms, but I came again, and when I arched up, he slipped inside of me and showed me just how good those muscular thighs and butt were for thrusting. On his knees, he gripped my hips, angled my lower body up more, and found an angle I didn't think I'd ever experienced.

I came twice in a row, which made him growl in pride.

"I want to take longer, but I can't." He bent down and kissed my neck, the opposite side to what Kirk had marked, and licked softly. Increasing the depth of his thrusts, he carefully built up my orgasm right until his knot was fully inside of me. We both came and he bit my neck, marking me, and binding the three of us fully together.

"Finally!" I screamed as the hole in my heart filled with the three men I'd been longing for, for so long.

CHAPTER 26

Kirk

"Are you sure you want to do this?" Buck asked Brooklyn for the third time that afternoon.

She rolled her eyes. "I have to meet them sometime, so why not now?"

"Meeting them separately would be better," he explained. "They're a lot to handle ... *a lot*."

"Are you embarrassed by me?" she asked, and put her hands on her hips, her eyes narrowed in mock anger.

Thanks to the bond, we were able to sense her actual feelings and she was, thankfully, not angry or upset right now.

"Yep," Tyler said. "Absolutely mortified that our mate is so fucking gorgeous, strong, and independent."

"Be prepared to have them ask when you want babies," I said.

"Tomorrow," she answered with a nod of her head. "Any other questions?"

I growled and my dick twitched in my pants. "Don't

make promises like that, or I'll take you up to the nest, and we won't leave until there's a baby in your belly."

She batted her eyelashes and looked up at me innocently. "Oh, no. Anything, but that, *Alpha*."

She said alpha in a higher voice, knowing I liked it.

I growled again, but Tyler put his arm around her shoulders and steered her out of the room. "Let's go, or you're going to learn how real that threat of his was."

"I agree with Kirk. Let's keep her here, in the nest, and they can meet her when she's pregnant," Buck growled.

Tyler shook his head. "Silly alphas, don't you know that your mothers would beat down the door if you don't show up tonight?"

He was right, but still ...

"Fine," I grumbled and followed them out to the SUV.

Thankfully, Brooklyn wasn't anywhere near her heat or her pheromones likely would have had me following up on that promise.

"Are your dads going to be there, too?" Brooklyn asked and looked over her shoulder at Buck and I.

Buck nodded. "Yes, they all gather like this on occasion. They've become friends, since we were friends and became a pack."

"They actually stayed in contact and spent time together even when we were separated," I admitted.

"So, if one of them doesn't like me, then they all won't?" she asked softly, a hint of nervousness seeping through the bond.

"They're going to love you," I replied immediately and grabbed her into a hug.

"They'll just be excited we have our omega," Tyler said. "They've been waiting for this for decades."

"My family is going to be super excited to meet you guys as well," she said, and rubbed her face against my arm. "I should probably text them at least to let them know I'm mated now. If I do, though, they'll call me and demand all kinds of information and details that will wear me out before we make it to the dinner, so I think I'll wait and text them tomorrow."

"We could take a picture together and send it to them," Buck offered.

"I'd like a picture together," she said and looked at Tyler. "Is ... is that going to be okay? Your fans won't get upset that you're now off the market?"

"I don't give a shit what they or my marketing team will say. I'm going to post about it as soon as you tell us we can. I mean, I already wrote a song about you and admitted my love for you when I wrote my social media posts that are scheduled to go out in a few days. Now I can update those posts to say you're mine officially."

She stopped walking, her entire body tensed, and stared at him. "You ... you wrote a song about me?"

He smiled wide and nodded. "When you went shopping, that was the song I was recording. You re-inspired me, my little muse." He tapped the tip of her nose with a goofy smirk on his face.

She stepped forward, making me drop my arm, and hugged him. "How did I get so lucky?"

"We don't question the gods," I told her and hugged her

back. "We just thank them for giving us this second chance with you."

Buck joined our hug, his arms around Tyler and my backs. "You're our greatest gift in the universe."

"I love you guys," she said in a soft whisper.

All of our eyes met over the top of her head, wide and surprised.

"I love you, too," I said quickly.

"I've always loved you," Tyler said and kissed her head. "I was too stupid to realize it sooner."

"I love you as well," Buck said and kissed her cheek.

Huddled together, I felt my soul finally settle. This was exactly what I wanted ... needed. She was our missing piece, finally here to fill it and give us the peace we had been seeking.

And we were here to give her that peace and fulfillment she had been missing. No matter what happened, we would be there for each other and never separate again. Never.

CHAPTER 27
Brooklyn

Two weeks after we became officially bonded, I signed papers to make Marcus half owner of the business. This also meant I was able to give him more of the responsibilities, move in with my pack, and focus on further developing our emotional bonds.

My father had nearly fainted when I called him and told him I was mated. He thought I'd been pranking him until Kirk took the phone and spoke to him. Mother was overjoyed and demanded to visit us, unless we visited her soon. I'd agreed to take the guys to meet them next month, after we'd had more time alone. The guys would love my parents' place and we could explore the sights for a mini vacation.

Their mothers and fathers had scrambled over each other to embrace me when we had arrived for that first dinner. My worry about them liking me had truly been for naught. They were so happy the boys had found me.

Tyler's mom had ripped into him when she found out

we'd known each other in high school and his antics had caused our separation.

I did agree with him, though, it had been good for us to follow our own paths for a bit, to come into our own as adults with our own businesses and events that developed us into the people we were today. Now, we were inseparable.

More often than not, we were in the nest, sleeping together instead of in our own rooms. I absolutely loved it. Each morning, one of them would make breakfast, and although I wasn't going through a midlife crisis anymore, they still made me mimosas on the weekends.

Tyler even bought me a sports car I'd been drooling over, much to Buck and Kirk's irritation since it was a "safety risk."

I loved driving the fast, little car around town.

"I still can't believe that you signed half the company to me," Marcus said, and swallowed hard as he stared at the signed, notarized, and official documents before him.

"You're my best friend and probably the only reason this business even did so well, if I'm being honest. You deserve it. Plus, I want to spend less time working."

"And more time boinking," he said, and waggled his eyebrows.

I pushed his shoulder and laughed. "Well, if I am going to have a child, I need to make that happen as soon as possible. I'm not getting any younger."

"You do look more beautiful now that you're packed up," he said with a soft smile.

"Speaking of packing up ... how's it going with your new pack?"

He flushed. "We started courting this adorable omega;

apparently, she used to work at that resort you found the guys at. What a small world, right?"

"What's her name?" I asked, curious.

"Ana."

My mouth dropped. "The waitress? Oh my gosh, she is amazing and sweet, and I totally approve."

He rolled his eyes. "Glad you approve, Mom."

"Anyway, you know you can call me anytime you need something, right? I'm not trying to drop this on you and run away, but I'd rather not fly out here if necessary."

"That's what we have videoconferencing for," he agreed. "I really am super happy for you, Brooklyn. It's amazing that you found each other after so long."

"Hey, babe," Kirk said as he walked into the conference room. "You get everything all official?"

Marcus raised the documents. "Signed and sealed, Kirk-y boy!"

Kirk shook his head at my rambunctious best friend. "Glad to hear it. So, that means we can steal her away to finish packing?"

I groaned. "I don't wanna!" I shouted in a childlike tantrum.

"You only have your office left," Kirk reminded me and kissed my cheek as he came to stand beside me. "It won't take that long."

"Oh! Do I get your office now?" Marcus asked, eyes wide with excitement.

"No!" I shouted, but immediately sighed and nodded. "Yes, yes you do."

He pumped his fist in the air. "Fuck yes! Hurry and go with your mate to get your shit out of my office."

Laughing and shaking my head, I stood and tugged a bit of his hair. "Brat."

"You love me," he said in a sing-song voice.

Kirk growled, but quickly stopped it.

"I do, but you push your limits sometimes. Anyway, call me if you need anything, okay? I know the next launch is ready and just waiting for the appropriate timing."

"And I'll schedule the video meetings for the brain dumping sessions for the next launch. I know you had a few ideas you hadn't shared yet, which I'm hoping to incorporate in future launches."

"Oh, I've got a ton of ideas," I said with a nod, and followed Kirk towards the door.

Marcus followed behind and fidgeted with the papers for a second. "I am going to miss you."

I hugged him and patted his back. "You're welcome to come to the ranch anytime you need a break. Maybe we can make a quarterly owners' retreat, so you can come find new launch ideas and take a mini vacation. What do you think?"

He hugged me tighter and nodded. "I think that sounds great."

We pulled back and I winked. "And maybe one of these times you'll bring Ana with you."

He rubbed the back of his neck and smiled. "Fingers crossed, girl. Fingers crossed."

After an hour of packing and grumbling, we walked out of the office with two boxes of things, and down to the parking garage, where Tyler and Buck waited for us.

"Ready?" Tyler asked as they loaded my things.

I nodded and smiled at my three mates: Tyler, my happy rockstar. Buck, my confident athlete. Kirk, my teddy bear marine. They were everything I could have wanted and more.

This was my happily ever after, and I was so glad I got to experience it with them, even if I'd had to wait longer than most.

"Yeah, I'm ready," I agreed with a nod and a wide smile.

If you enjoyed this book, you might also enjoy the Accidental Mobster Series, a complete light contemporary mafia RH romance series full of sass, laughs, and fun: **books2read.com/accidental-mobster**.

Don't forget to join my newsletter for deals, snippets, and giveaways: **catbanks.co/newsletter**

About the Author

Daisy Emory is the contemporary romance pseudonym for Catherine Banks, USA Today Bestselling Author.

amazon.com/author/daisyemory

About the Author

Catherine Banks is a USA Today bestselling fantasy author who writes in several fantasy subgenres and has multiple pseudonyms. She began writing fiction at only four years old and finished her first full-length novel at the age of fifteen. She is married to her soulmate and best friend, Avery, who she has two amazing children with. After her full-time job, she reads books, plays video games, and watches anime shows and movies with her family to relax. Although she has lived in Northern California her entire life, she dreams of traveling around the world. Catherine is also C.E.O. of Turbo Kitten Industries™, a company with many hats including being a book publisher and Etsy store full of nerdy fun.

facebook.com/catherinebanksauthor

amazon.com/author/catherinebanks

bookbub.com/authors/catherine-banks